HER DIRTY JOCKS

A MEN AT WORK ROMANCE

MIKA LANE

HEADLANDS PUBLISHING

COPYRIGHT

Copyright© 2021 by Mika Lane
Headlands Publishing
4200 Park Blvd. #244
Oakland, CA 94602

Her Dirty Jocks is a work of fiction. Names, characters, (most) places, and incidents are either the product of the author's creativity or are used fictitiously. Any resemblance to actual persons, living or dead, events, or locales is entirely coincidental.
All rights reserved. This book or any portion thereof may not be reproduced or used in any manner whatsoever without the express written permission of the publisher except for the use of quotations in a book review.

BE THE FIRST TO KNOW...

Want more heat, heart,
and bad boys who know what they're doing?
Join my list and I'll send the steam straight to your inbox,
starting with a deliciously naughty story:

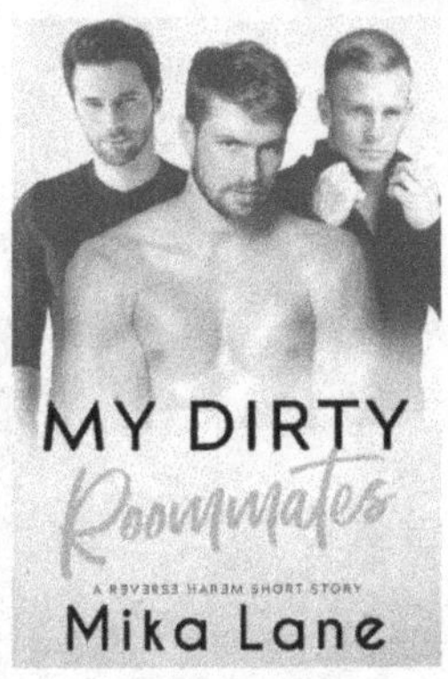

SIGN UP TO MY MAILING LIST!
Or visit:
https://geni.us/free-book-signup

FRANCES (FRANKI) CRAWFORD

"THAT'S NOT GOING TO WORK FOR ME."

The head of the campus tutoring center gave me a look that said, in no uncertain terms, that he couldn't give a shit about what *did* or *did not* work for me.

That's when I knew I had a problem.

I looked at the slip of paper he'd given me, my first assignment as a tutor, and found the guy I was assigned to help drag his lazy ass through statistics class was none other than State football star Garrett Stevens, someone I'd not known until last week.

If you wanted to be technical, I still didn't really know him.

Although I'd slept with him.

Yup, after having a rough couple days that included premenstrual horniness, needing rebound sex to forget the douchebag I'd dated over the summer, and feeling generally pissed off at the world, I indulged in one of those sleazy rite of passage one-night stands that college is famous for.

That's all it was. Seriously.

"Um, Max if you could match me up with another student, I'd really appreciate it," I said, doing my best to sound breezy and casual while boob sweat collected in my bra.

He studied me, trying to read between the lines. Finally, he sighed. "Franki, you signed up to work here two weeks into the semester. That's about three weeks later than everybody else. You don't get your pick of students to work with. Sorry."

He clicked his computer keyboard one more time and looked at me with a forced smile that indicated it was time for me to get the hell out of his office.

I was getting desperate, and because of that, wasn't above begging. Or flattering.

"I know you're super busy, Max, and I hate to keep you from your work, especially at the beginning of a semester. But this is kind of important."

That should drag some empathy out of his tired, overworked ass.

Who knew a campus tutoring center would be such

a hubbub of activity? I supposed if you used tutoring services, you'd know that well. But since I was a pretty good student who managed to muddle my way through even the worst of the classes that made up my freshman year, and who'd never needed a tutor, it was all new to me.

Also new to me this year was taking on a job to pay for school. Mom and Dad were flat out of money, leaving me to scramble for student loans and part-time work. Tutoring was one of the best-paying jobs on campus, and the director let me know that by working with student athletes, I'd actually get paid a little extra.

I couldn't say no to that. Next semester's tuition bill was coming like a freight train, and the financial assistance my parents had offered my older brother and sister for their schooling, dried up just in time for me to hit my freshman year. Now that I'd entered my sophomore year, their situation wasn't getting any better. I was pretty much on my own.

Lucky me.

Yeah, my fortunate siblings had gotten fully-paid rides to private universities. Me, not so much. By the time my turn came, Dad was ready to retire. My parents had spent almost their last cent on my brother and sister, so it was decided I would attend State, which was loads cheaper.

I wasn't bitter. Really.

Even when faced with having to tutor a burly football player who I just happened to have gotten down and dirty with not one week earlier.

I'd thought I was so smart. Figured I'd never see him again. After all, State was one of those universities bigger than some towns. You could get lost, stay anonymous, keep your head down, and hardly ever see the same person twice.

How was it then that I was now faced with having to tutor the one guy on campus I'd fucked in a moment of sexy weakness?

Thinking I was clever, I'd left my panties behind, hanging on his bedroom doorknob. Show him how the cool girls do it. Give him something to think about because he was never going to see my ass again. I lied about my major, which dorm I lived in, where I came from, you name it. I hadn't even given him my real name, instead pretending to be a Susan. Seemed sufficiently bland enough to be forgettable.

I hadn't lied about the orgasms, though. They were quite something. And god knew I needed them.

Not that he asked for it, but I wouldn't have given him my contact info, anyway. Like he would have ever called me. Guys like him were famous for ghosting. So I beat him to the punch. Used him before he could use me, and all that.

And at the time, I'd felt pretty good about it.

Now, not so much.

Max sighed when he looked up from his computer

monitor to see I was still sitting there. "Franki, you are right. I am busy," he said impatiently.

"Max, I… I don't think I can work with Garrett Stevens."

He frowned. "Why? Is he an ex or something?"

Should I tell Max I'd fucked the guy and really didn't want to have to make nice with him and that, oh by the way, I couldn't stand jocks, anyway? That they were creeps with little or no interest in academics, who also had jumped my brother in high school and pummeled the shit out of him?

I could hold a grudge. I wasn't proud of it.

"No. He's not an ex," I said, keeping my drama to myself.

Satisfaction settled on his face. "Great. Then you will be tutoring three students on the subject of statistics." He wrinkled his nose. "God, I always hated stats. Too bad I didn't have someone like you to help me out back in the day. I'm sure I would have been motivated to study my ass off."

Looking me up and down, he gave me a giant, smarmy grin and waited for me to thank him for his cheesy compliment.

I stood to leave, holding my backpack in front of me to limit his hungry gaze. "I guess some people just aren't smart enough for stats."

Ooh. Did I really just say that?

His smile faded. "Well, it's not that—"

But I didn't hear the rest of what he had to say.

I'd gotten the work I needed to make it through the semester and pay for at least part of the next. I was out of there.

I'd tutor Garrett Stevens, even if all I could think about the whole time was how talented his tongue was…

"Whattup, Frank?" my BFF Daniel said, answering my call before the first ring had even finished.

I took a seat on the front steps of the student union, Daniel's voice nearly drowned out by the buzz of giggly undergrads, beleaguered professors, creaky university shuttle buses, and rumbling food trucks.

"Hey. I got a job tutoring stats," I told him.

"Wow, look at the big brain on my girl," he screeched.

God, I missed him. We'd had a fun summer, and I'd almost cried when I left for school and he stayed behind.

Said college just wasn't his thing. Driving for Uber was about as far as his ambition went.

"Big brain, you're so funny. But get this. My first student is that guy I had the one-nighter with last week. Doesn't it just figure?"

A couple heads snapped in my direction at the mention of 'one-nighter.'

"That's what happens when you're a ho," Daniel said

gleefully. "I hope he at least had a good-sized dick, honey."

In the background, I heard a turn signal click-click-click and realized he was driving.

"Dan, you don't have anyone in the car with you, do you? You know, a passenger who might be listening to you talking about big dicks."

Discretion was not one of his strengths.

He cackled. "I most certainly do, Frances Mary Crawford. Just so happens I have a couple ladies I'm taking to their card game at the senior center. Everything good back there, girls?" he called.

I didn't hear them respond.

"Okay, Dan, I'm gonna run. But you might try to keep your conversations rated G, at least when you have passengers."

"Oh, honey, everyone likes the booty. Don't be ashamed. You did nothing wrong."

Easy for him to say. He was a walking one-night stand.

Besides, if I had nothing to be embarrassed about, why was I dreading facing Garrett Stevens?

FRANKI

"Hey, Mom," I said, once back in my dorm room where there was more quiet.

"Oh, Frances, hi," she said.

"*Honey, it's Frances on the line,*" she hollered to my dad, having pulled the receiver only slightly away from her mouth.

"I got the tutoring job," I said like somebody had died.

She clicked her tongue. "Don't sound so excited, Frances."

I wanted to ask her how excited *she'd* be, having to abandon all hope of attending a prestigious university

—and to add insult to injury, having to scrape together tuition money that my older brother and sister never had to trouble themselves with?

I didn't mean to sound like an entitled shit, but it was hard not to compare my situation to my siblings'.

Breathless, my dad came on the line. "Hi, Franny, was just cleaning out the attic. Hey, Mom and I are looking at RVs. There are some really cool ones out there. We figure we'll drive around the country for a year or two to celebrate my retirement. Then, maybe I'll get a hobby job or something. You know, like as a docent at a museum or something. Part-time only, of course." He laughed like a man who knew the taste of freedom was just around the corner.

I was glad my parents were planning the next phase of their lives. They'd worked hard to raise us kids, and deserved every bit of happiness and fun that came their way.

I just wished I'd had some warning that they were going to pull the plug just as I was heading to college. When they'd realized they couldn't afford a third private school tuition after paying for my brother and sister, I'd scrambled to get into State. They'd covered most of my freshman year, but now that I was a sophomore, I was footing the bill pretty much alone.

Which was fine. I was making it all work.

"Your mother told me you got a job. Congratulations. You know, Franny," Dad continued, "this is going to be a big character-builder for you, in a way that your older brother and sister didn't have. I often wonder if they had it a little too easy…" He trailed off.

I would have *liked* to have had the chance to have it too easy. But I kept my smart-assed thoughts to myself.

"So, Dad, my job is tutoring a *football player*." I could barely spit the words out.

He drew a deep breath, and I knew his voice of reason was coming. "Well now, Franny, they deserve your help just like any other student does—"

But I cut him off. "We all know, Dad, they are not exactly there for the academics," I said self-righteously.

Max had explained to me, further cementing my resentment of jocks and dislike of sports in general, that athletes' tutoring needs were prioritized above all others. It was my job to keep the guy I'd be helping eligible to play and that the extra pay I'd get was for the inevitable challenge of doing that. Max didn't come out and say so, but the implication was clear—tutoring a football player was not going to be an easy job. He'd need a lot of help for a variety of reasons, not least of which, I was assuming, was questionable interest in his classes.

"What are you teaching, Franny?" Dad asked, eager to avoid an argument.

"Stats." Not a subject I loved—hell, who *did* love stats?—but it was one of the few subjects left where they still needed tutors.

Lucky for me, a lot of people needed help with stats.

Dad knew my general dislike of jocks stemmed in part from my brother's experience. He didn't know, of course, that my specific objection to one Garrett Stevens was our thoughtless and poorly planned tryst the first week back on campus for the new school year.

Which I now regretted on the level of cutting my own bangs.

Badly-cut bangs would eventually go away. A one-night stand would not.

3

GARRETT STEVENS

My instructor floated up and down the aisles of our classroom, plunking graded quizzes on our desks. Face down.

She was having fun. Maybe more fun than she'd ever had in her life. Guess that's how stats instructors rolled.

But fun for her did not mean fun for me.

I held my breath and flipped my paper over. There it was.

A big, fat, fucking *F*.

Written in cheerful Christmas red with a big-ass circle around it.

And a little note underneath to see her after class.

I wasn't surprised, but that didn't mean it still didn't hurt. I didn't get a lot of bad grades, fortunately, being a mostly C to B guy, like a lot of student athletes. In fact, this was my first F ever. And from my discreet glances around the classroom, I wasn't the only one who flunked the first stats quiz of the semester. In fact, I think I saw a couple tears dribble down the face of the girl at the desk next to mine. Couldn't blame her. I wouldn't have minded shedding a couple tears, myself.

If I were the crying kind of guy. Which I was not.

Why Statistics 101 was a required core course was beyond me. It was a miserable subject offering nothing practical, at least from what I could tell.

Of course, it didn't help that my football training schedule left me a minimal amount of time to devote to my studies. It didn't help that a subject as cryptic as stats definitely got the short end of the stick when it came to study time.

But if I didn't pull my grade up in this class, my entire football career would be getting the short end of the stick.

The teacher blew through the day's lecture, building on the material that half the class—myself included— had failed to master as proven by our lousy quiz grades. Speaking for myself, I was more frustrated than ever and convinced that an F on my first quiz was a bellwether for what was to come.

"You wanted to see me?" I asked after the rest of the class had pretty much filed out, defeated as we were.

She tilted her head, looking at me with a maternal smile. Which made the rest of our conversation that much more skeevy.

"Mr. Stevens—or may I call you Garrett?" she asked.

"Garrett is fine."

I wasn't even sure of *her* name.

She propped her butt on the edge of the desk as students for the next class began to filter in.

She'd better hurry. I didn't need a roomful of people knowing one of State's star football players was struggling with a class I should have tackled back when I was a freshman. I'd put off taking it long enough and now that I was a senior, things were down to the wire.

"Garrett," she said quietly, looking me up and down and settling on my biceps, "I contacted your coach about your grade. I had to. I'm sorry, and wanted you to know before you heard about it from him."

I nodded. "Yes, I know that's required of you."

"Have you signed up for help yet? The tutoring center has a lot of very qualified students waiting and ready for people like you."

People like me? What did that mean? Dumbasses who couldn't fake their way through a class that wasn't all multiple-choice?

"I am signed up. Starting tomorrow, in fact."

"Good, good," she purred, reaching out to touch me.

At first I thought she wanted to offer comfort, not that I needed it. But then I realized she was copping a feel when she ran a finger up my arm, stopping to caress my biceps.

Really?

Even after three years of playing football, the fascination women—and some guys—had with football players still blew my mind. It was the weirdest fucking thing and one I wasn't sure I'd ever get used to.

A lot of players loved it, and the endless pussy that came with it.

Me, not so much.

It wasn't that I didn't love a beautiful, sexy woman —which this instructor of mine was *not*—but the novelty of having women throw themselves at me for the status of fucking an athlete had worn off long ago.

Coach had warned us from day one—many of these women didn't give a shit about us—they just wanted to be able to say they'd been with an athlete, and the higher profile, the better.

And I was one of the highest profile players at the entire school. Well, after the team's quarterbacks. They were the *real* stars of the game.

It was a status thing, I'd been told. And it made me kind of sad. It all felt a little pathetic. Some of my teammates were the biggest douchebags I'd ever met. I cringed for the women who ripped off their panties to spend time with guys who wouldn't remember their names the next day, if they ever even thought to ask for them in the first place.

I didn't mean to sound like a self-righteous prick, but I'd been with a woman named Susan just the week before, who I *did* want to call again. Unfortunately, she'd hightailed it out of my dorm room the next morning before I'd woken up.

And she'd strangely left her panties behind, hanging on my doorknob so I couldn't miss them. What the hell did she think I'd want those for?

I backed away discreetly, beyond the instructor's reach, pretending to rifle through a notebook, which gave me a moment to look up her name.

Stephanie Miller.

"Miss Miller—"

She laughed softly. "Please, Garrett, call me Stephanie."

She scooted close again, and her hand returned to my arm. Cripes, she was persistent. "Look, I'm glad you're getting tutoring, but know that I'm here for you. Anything you need. Anything," she stressed with wide-open eyes.

Why didn't she just spread her legs and ask me to fuck her right there in front of the rapidly-filling classroom?

I nodded and stuffed my things into my backpack. "Thanks, Stephanie. I appreciate that."

"And one more thing, Garrett. If you ever have any

extra… game tickets, know that I love football. I mean, *really* love football."

Okay. Got it. Stephanie Miller, mediocre-at-best statistics teacher, loved football.

Although I wasn't sure what I could do for her. Faculty could attend games just like anybody else. She didn't need anything from me.

Coach's words ran through my head. He'd had us practice them until they flowed without any thought. Like right now. "I'm glad to know you're a fan. The team appreciates your support."

Those words were designed to get us out of any number of sticky situations we found ourselves in.

But the expression on her face tweaked when she realized I was just giving her our boilerplate brush off.

She decided to let me know how unhappy I'd just made her.

In a huff, she gathered her things. "Tell me, Garrett. I'd guess that playing football is pretty important to you."

Shit. This wasn't going to be good.

She frowned. "Well, *is* it?"

Here it comes. "Yes. Yes, it is," I said, my mouth dry.

"And I bet you'd do just about anything to ensure your continued spot on the team, right?"

Did she *have* to fuck with me? Couldn't I just wallow in my shitty grade and be done with it? She had to point out the power she had over me?

Satisfied by my silence, she smiled. "Okay. Thought so. We'll work together—*closely* together—to make sure you sail through this class. I *promise*, okay?" she said, her gaze drilling mine.

It didn't take a genius to read between the lines, and understand that recovering from my F wasn't going to be just a matter of acing the next quiz. I wasn't sure what she was holding out for. I didn't want to know.

And it didn't matter because whatever she was gunning for was never going to happen. She didn't know that yet, but she would soon.

The following class's instructor arrived and threw his things down on the desk where Stephanie Miller had planted one of her ass cheeks. "Hey, guys. You need to vacate, okay?" he said firmly.

My guess was that he was a stats teacher, as well. They clearly had no heart.

4

GARRETT

As I arrived for my first tutoring session, I found myself hoping I didn't end up with some man-eating female like my stats teacher who'd help me only on the condition that I do something for her—particularly something of a carnal nature. Second, I hoped I didn't get some dude who had an axe to grind against student athletes or who thought the school football team sucked.

If I did end up with one of these, I'd have to suck it up anyway. I needed my damn grade. I stood outside the student union for a couple minutes, weighing my options, while nearly every female who passed me stared and smiled.

I was so not in the mood.

Fuck. I had to go inside. Not to would be career suicide. If I failed a class—any class—my spot on the team would be in jeopardy, along with my free ride at the university.

To throw that away would be about the stupidest thing I could ever do. So, I hoisted my backpack onto my shoulder without thinking, and nearly fell to my knees in searing pain.

Fortunately, I was right next to a handrail, which I grabbed before anyone could see that one of the school's star athletes had an injury he was hiding.

My shoulder was seriously fucked. I needed treatment. But to ask for it would bring a shit show of trouble down on my head.

I dropped my pack back to the ground while I waited for the knife-sharp pain to dissipate. This one had been bad, and in fact had not only taken my breath away, but also brought stinging tears to my eyes.

When I could see straight again, I hoisted my pack onto my good shoulder and made my way inside.

"I'm Franki Crawford," a black-haired woman said, extending her hand before even looking up at me from her laptop.

And when she finally did, we both stopped in our tracks.

Oh.

Great. This was just great. But it fit with the rest of my day, so why should the universe stop layering another load of crap on me now?

I took her hand. "Um. Hi. I'm Garrett Stevens."

She glared at me as I took a seat. "When we met last week, I told you my name was Susan."

Dear god, please don't let this one be a bunny boiler. I just didn't have the stomach for a psycho today.

"Well, it's not," she continued.

"Um, yeah, I kind of figured. Franki. Where'd you get a name like that?" I asked, hoping to cut some of the chill in the room.

She pressed her lips together. "My given name is Frances."

Holy shit. She did not look like a Frances.

I wouldn't take someone with her punky rock 'n roll vibe for a Frances.

She clicked around on her computer, throwing me some world-class side-eye.

"Look, if this is too awkward, I can request another tutor—" I started to say.

"Actually, you can't request another tutor. You're stuck with me."

Which I guessed was another way of saying *she* was stuck with *me*.

Fine.

Keep your eye on the ball, and all that.

"Look, um—"

"*Franki.* The name is Franki," she said, rolling her eyes.

"Yeah, Franki, I know that," I said, wondering what I'd been thinking the night I hooked up with her, "I need to get a C or better in my stats class."

When she still didn't look up from her laptop, I decided to go in for the kill. "I'll give you your panties back. If you want them."

Bingo.

First, she turned pink. Then red. Then what could qualify as purple, usually seen only when someone was choking to death.

Shit. Maybe she *was* choking.

She coughed a couple times.

Dude. Don't fucking kill the girl.

"Very funny," she said.

It wasn't my fault she was short on a sense of humor. She'd seemed cool when we hooked up at one of the campus dive bars.

She was hot in a bad-girl, take-no-shit sort of way, something I didn't come across often in my day-to-day at State. I was usually surrounded by preppy blondes, not artsy types, and I was intrigued. And fuck if she wasn't a maniac in bed. In fact, I'd been jerking off to her memory all week, remembering how I'd pushed her over the edge as I screwed her brains out.

I think what I'd liked best was that she didn't give a shit who I was. No fawning, no bowing and scraping. I liked that. It was new for me.

When she was gone the next morning, I'd written the whole thing off as one of those nights where two people needed each other, got their rocks off, and went their separate ways.

Nothing more, nothing less.

And here we were now, our paths having crossed once more.

We needed each other again. I needed her knowledge, and I assumed she needed whatever she was getting paid for her time.

We were evenly matched. No imbalance.

But if that were the case, then why the hell did I feel like I was in the one-down position? I wasn't playing a damn football game.

Some people didn't like jocks, but this one was over the top. Have you ever sat in front of a beautiful woman who looked at you like she hated your fucking guts?

5

FRANKI

"Garrett. Hey, Garrett?"

My new student, who also happened to be my first-ever student, was staring off into space, probably remembering the hot night we'd spent together, while I was trying to teach him the fascinating principles of statistics.

Believe me, I knew it wasn't the most exciting of subjects. In fact, it was probably one of the most miserable. I'd hated it, but I'd also been strangely good at it.

For some archaic reason, State required everyone take at least one semester of stats, which created ample job opportunities for someone like me. Because the subject was pretty much universally loathed, a lot of people needed help with it.

Yay, me.

Still, it would be nice if Garrett could pay attention during the scant hour we were scheduled to spend together. To be honest, I didn't want to be there any more than he did. I'd rather be taking care of my own schoolwork than helping someone else with theirs.

But there we were. And he'd better fucking listen. We'd both look bad if he didn't pull his stats grade up— he could get kicked off the football team for a too-low GPA, and I could get kicked out of one of the few decently-paying college jobs.

Which would mean the end of my own college career. So really, we needed to help each other. I was about to spell all that out when he snapped back to attention.

"Right. Yeah. Sorry," he said, shaking the cobwebs from his brain.

"Can you pull out your book, homework, and any other stuff you have?" I asked.

He reached into his backpack. First, he handed me something face down. When I turned it over, I saw it was a failed quiz. Then, he opened his book to the day's lecture, and last, showed me the study problems the instructor had assigned.

"Okay," I said, assessing the situation.

I saw right off the bat that Garrett just needed to

get a few of the basics down and that he'd probably be fine after that.

"You know, we're only a couple weeks into the semester. Why don't we start at the beginning of the book, try and catch up really fast, and then it will be easier to stay on top of things for the rest of the semester

He nodded. "Sounds great."

He looked anything but great. In fact, he looked pretty miserable.

Was he trying to get me to feel sorry for him? Because it wasn't going to work. Everyone at State had to pass stats. There was no way around it. No amount of pressure from the football coach or anyone else was going to pass this class for anyone. It was one of those things you just had to suck up.

"This class is killing me. I can't get my head around it. Did you find it hard when you took it?" he asked.

I thought about how to answer. I wanted to bitch about stats like every normal person did, but at the same time didn't want to discourage him.

"I wouldn't say I liked it. But what made it bearable was that I had a teacher who not only taught the principles but also put them in context. So, I'm a psychology major, and psych does a lot of studies and stuff. What I did was try to imagine how I would use them in research. That helped a lot."

He studied me. "A psych major. Why am I not surprised?"

"Well," I said, "contrary to popular belief, not all psych majors are nymphos. That night I was with you was just a fluke. I don't do that all the time."

"I didn't think you did."

Oh. Right.

Guess I was being harder on myself than anyone around me. But I had a tendency to do that.

"Let's get started," I said, flipping to the start of the book. "Why don't you read the first problem to me?"

But strangely, he just stared at the page, his lips moving the tiniest amount.

I gave him another moment.

"Everything okay, Garrett?" I asked.

He nodded slowly.

"Okay," I said. "Here. I'll read it and we'll work through it together."

After going through a couple practice problems, he got the third one right. And then the fourth and fifth.

Maybe I had a knack for this teaching stuff.

Or maybe Garrett was smart and just needed a good teacher.

But his avoiding reading from his textbook was strange.

"Damn. This stuff is starting to make sense," he said, shaking his head in disbelief. "Never thought that would happen."

He looked at me and smiled, his boy next door looks belying the hugeness of his physique. It was almost like his face didn't match his body. And somehow the effect was cute. Really cute.

Guess that's why I'd done… what I'd done with him.

We continued like that until five minutes to the hour—I'd read a problem and he would talk through how to solve it.

His mood, heavy and dark when he'd arrived, was tons lighter.

I had to admit I was having fun, too. It felt good to see such fast results. It also felt good to help someone who was willing to learn.

"Holy crap. Thank you, Franki. I'm amazed." His brown eyes were sincere.

And amazing.

Ugh. Calm down, girl.

I wasn't sure who was happier about his breakthrough. After all, it was the first time I'd ever tutored anyone. I'd had no illusion that it would be a slam dunk.

"Shit. Look at the time." He stuffed his things into his backpack. "Practice starts in twenty minutes. I gotta run. But Franki, why don't you let me give you tickets to an upcoming home game? I get two per game that the guys usually give to their parents. But my parents hardly ever come. So you can have them."

Crap. I didn't want to insult him, but attending a

football game was pretty close to the last thing I wanted to do on a Saturday.

"C'mon. Please accept them," he said as he started to head out.

I waved him off. "Don't waste the tickets on me. I don't know the first thing about football."

He thrust his phone at me. "Here. Put your number in my phone. Please. I'll email you the tickets. And don't worry about not knowing the game. You'll get the gist of what's going on from the people in the stands."

"Well, okay, I guess. But I'm telling you, they will serve someone else much better."

No way I was freaking going.

"Bring your... roommate or someone," he suggested.

Now that was an idea. Maddy was star-struck by football players. It was the most unfathomably stupid thing, being obsessed with oversized human beings who beat the shit out of each other on a big green field. Wait till she found out I was tutoring a player.

He hoisted his backpack onto a shoulder and took off.

But strangely, before he did, he winced with pain.

I WAS tired from my session with Garrett, but it was good tired. I'd really accomplished something, and it was freaking great. I mean, yeah, I wanted the guy to get a decent grade in his class so he could keep playing football. But it also felt good to know I had enough knowledge to explain to someone else the subject-from-hell.

Never knew I had it in me.

On my way out, I stopped to check the next day's schedule. "Max, I'm signed up to work again tomorrow, right?" I asked. "Another new student?"

He scrolled through his computer. "Yeah... let me see. Oh. A football player named...Zane Rafferty."

No. Way. He hadn't told me I was the stats go-to for college athletes.

Things had gone well with Garrett, but that was a fluke. No way would things go that smoothly with another jock.

"What? Another one? Why?" I moaned.

He rolled his eyes at me. "Hey, if you don't want this job, I am sure someone else would be glad to snatch it up. On the other hand, not too many people can stomach stats. So maybe I'd better be nice to you." He cackled at his joke.

Shit. Garrett had actually been great as soon as we got over the initial embarrassment of remembering we'd seen each other naked. And he'd caught on to the material quickly and gotten the work done after a bit of explaining, even though he'd strangely avoided reading the problems out loud. But who's to say the next football player would be like him?

"Stop scowling, please," Max said. "Look, the athletic department is very committed to making sure these guys get decent grades."

I didn't see why the university didn't place the same importance on the education of all its students. But I kept that to myself.

Anyone could use the tutoring center, it was true. But there was no hand holding of your average student at State. No one watching to make sure you did okay. Actually, no one gave a crap if you fell flat on your ass.

That was a big state university for you.

And yet. I'd hoped to tutor people who just needed a little boost—students who were really committed to their studies and appreciated the educational opportunities at their fingertips.

I supposed I could quit. But that would be cutting off my nose to spite my face. I needed money for next semester, and this was pretty much the only way to get it.

Like it or not, I was stuck with my two jocks. And they were stuck with me.

6

———

FRANKI

I WENT TO OPEN MY DORM ROOM DOOR, WHEN I HEARD the tell-tale moaning of an afternoon hook up coming from the other side of it. I stopped and leaned my head against the hallway's cinder block wall.

Shit. Who was she with now?

I knocked lightly.

"Oh, yeah, give it to me..." She groaned as bedsprings squeaked loudly.

Well, shit.

I had stuff to do, and that included getting into my room. I looked at my watch. I'd give her ten minutes and no more. After that point, I would start pounding on the door. I didn't care what the hell she was doing in there.

I sank to the floor outside my room and cracked open my abnormal psych book. Just as I was getting into personality disorders—my personal favorite—one of the guys from upstairs happened by.

"Franki. You locked out or something?" he asked.

I looked at him for a moment and realization crossed his face when he heard the moaning. "Oh. I see."

I shrugged. "What can you do?" I said, laughing as if I weren't getting pissed off. "Actually, I've been out here ten minutes. Time's up, girlfriend."

I stood, and with the heel of my hand, pounded on the door. "Maddy. I need to get in there."

Silence.

Amused, my upstairs neighbor went on about his business.

"I'm serious, Maddy. I have work to do." I pounded on the door again.

I never pulled shit like that on her.

Suddenly, the door blew open and a guy rushed out, still zipping his pants. He glanced my way and without really focusing, muttered, "Sorry," under his breath, and took off like his ass was on fire.

I picked up my things and went inside.

The place stunk.

"Goddamn, Maddy. I think you need to go to the

doctor or something," I said, running to open a window.

She hopped out of bed naked and pulled on her robe. "Oh relax. I was just… blowing off some steam. You should try it some time. It wouldn't kill you to get laid."

What she didn't know was that I had indeed gotten laid just the week before. And look where that got me. Embarrassed at my new job in front of my new tutoring student.

And down one pair of underwear.

She plopped down on her bed, cross-legged. "Look. I'm sorry. That was inconsiderate of me."

While we hadn't roomed together for long, I knew her well enough to know that her sudden change in tune probably meant she wanted something. All I had to do was be quiet and wait a moment and she'd reveal her true intentions.

"Franki, you know how I'm trying out for Jane Austen's *Pride and Prejudice*, right? This fall's drama department production?"

I looked at her with crossed arms, trying to stay mad, or at least look like I was. But who could be mad with Jane Austen on the mind?

Only my favorite author, ever.

"What about it?" I griped. I was trying to act pissed. I really was.

"Will you run my lines with me? I need to practice."

I looked at my watch. I supposed I could spare a few minutes. Actually, to feel like I was in a Jane Austen novel, I could spare a lot more than that.

"Okay," I said, eagerly. "Let's do it."

She jumped up and clapped her hands. "Oh goody. Okay, here is what I'm supposed to read for the audition."

She rifled through a stack of papers on her desk and pulled out a couple pages, thrusting one at me.

Oooh, it was one of my favorite scenes—the one where it's discovered that the youngest sister, Lydia Bennet, has run off with the creep George Wickham.

So juicy. And so wrong.

"Hey, Maddy, before we get started, want two tickets to a football game with me? I got two really good seats."

She stopped what she was doing and studied me. "Where'd you get those? The student section has some of the worst seats in the entire stadium."

"These aren't student seats. They are for real, grown up seats. I'm tutoring a football player, and he offered them for helping him."

Maddy's mouth dropped open, and she sank back onto her bed. "What the fucking fuck? You're tutoring a football player?"

I knew she'd be blown away. "Yeah. Actually, more than one. Seems they need a lot of help with stats."

Maddy rolled her eyes. "Well, everyone needs help with stats…"

I didn't need help.

"I'll tell you what. Of course I want to go. But—you have to come with me."

I shook my head. "No, it's a waste to use the tickets on me. I couldn't give a shit about football. Take both of them and invite someone else. Invite that guy you just fucked."

She waved her hand. "Ew, no. I won't be seeing him again. He's not into oral."

Oh. The non-kiss of death.

"Well, I'm not going, it's just not my thing—"

But Maddy cut me off. "Look, home games are a big part of college life. Come with me just this once. I'll explain the game to you, and I promise, it will be fun."

I shrugged. "Fine. Fine, but I'm telling you, don't be surprised if you see me reading a book on my phone when I get bored. Which will probably be about five minutes after the start."

She laughed. "Fair enough. Kudos to you for giving it a shot. Now… can you introduce me to your players?"

Shit. Of course she'd want to meet them.

"I don't really want to hang out with them. A bunch of jocks jumped my brother when he was in high school. I've never liked them since."

She waved away my concern. "Oh, get over it. We're in college now."

She had a point. But my opinion was not going to change anytime soon.

No matter how cute and charming Garrett Stevens was.

And how cute and charming my new student, Zane Rafferty, might be.

Yeah, I'd looked him up online. A girl had to be prepared, didn't she?

7

ZANE RAFFERTY

"Help yourself, Zane."

I popped a bite of steak into my mouth that the dining hall cook had slipped me and closed my eyes to savor it. "You've done it again, Hal. This is freaking awesome."

I wiped my hands clean on my apron and piled several freshly-grilled steaks into a chafing dish to bring them out to the football players' dining room.

Yup. We football players had our own dining room away from the other students and even other athletes, where we regularly ate high-end food like steak, roasted chicken, and the occasional piece of fish when the trainers thought we needed to broaden our horizons.

I'd never even set foot in one of the general dining halls.

Not that I was feeling all that privileged. While the rest of my team sat there stuffing their faces and trading war stories, guess who was busting his ass working?

Yup, me.

As a team walk-on, I got no scholarship money. Since my parents couldn't foot my tuition, room, and board bill, I had to work. So, I nabbed a job in the dining hall where I'd be eating anyway. Might as well kill two birds with one stone.

I lucked out when my grandmother paid for most of the year's expenses, something she'd agreed to do after I spent my first year at the local community college, proving myself with good grades. Bless her goddamn heart, she'd given me her life savings. I planned to pay it back of course, but the only way I could stay in school for my junior and senior year after this, was if I managed to get the coach to give me a scholarship.

Otherwise, I'd be out on my ass.

My dining hall job paid for books and some other incidentals but didn't come close to touching the big college bills.

But it wasn't so bad. The cook let me eat whatever I wanted, whenever I wanted.

I brought out a new tray of mashed potatoes and then refilled the salad. I never realized just how much football players ate until I looked at it from this perspective.

We were freaking bottomless pits.

"Dude. Can you take a break now?"

I looked up from the pots I was washing to see that my roommate Garrett had joined me in the kitchen. I turned off the water and dried my hands.

"Hal, I'm eating," I called. "Be back in fifteen."

He didn't look up from what he was doing, and instead just waved.

Garrett and I loaded our plates and took seats away from the rest of the guys. It wasn't that we didn't want to eat with them, but there were a couple obnoxious assholes we avoided when possible.

Like our quarterback, Atlas.

"Goddamn, this steak is good," Garrett said, wolfing his down.

"Seriously. Hal does a kick-ass job."

It helped that he was a huge football fan and we players regularly plied him with the best seats we could get. And it was totally worth it. He cooked almost better than my grandmother. Almost.

"Coach say anything about a scholarship for ya yet?" Garrett asked.

I wish.

"Nah. Too early. He hasn't seen me play enough. But I'm feeling good about it."

"Well, I guess next year is a long way off, anyway. But it never hurts to plan ahead. And I saw the tapes of your practice. They were damn good, buddy."

"Thanks."

My roommate Garrett was a good guy, and I was lucky we'd been matched together. And he was right about planning—if Coach didn't come through with a scholarship for me for next year, I'd be back at community college living at home again.

Sometimes I thought I should have just stayed there, at home, and not been so ambitious. Life would be so much simpler, and the constant worries about money would be minimal. And I'd be closer to my younger siblings, who I worried about pretty much day and night.

There was a commotion at the big table where a group of the players always ate. Garrett and I looked over to see Atlas throwing a dinner bun at another guy.

"Such a douche," I muttered.

Garrett leaned closer and lowered his voice. "Ah, he's not so bad. Just kind of clueless. You'll see. Give him a chance."

I wanted to. I really did. And I had to admit part of my issue with him probably stemmed from the green-eyed monster, jealousy.

Atlas Whitlowe had been given every opportunity in the world—every opportunity that had always been out of my reach, and which I'd kill to have. His father was loaded, he came from a football-playing legacy, and rumor had it he'd never worked a day in his life, although I wasn't sure I bought that one. Regardless, he was a star quarterback and strutted around campus like his shit didn't stink. It was said that at one point so many girls wanted to sleep with him that the team had to hire him security.

I was pretty sure that was an urban legend like so many things are, but still. To have even a rumor like that swirling around yourself was pretty fucking baller.

"I had my first meeting with my stats tutor," Garrett said, chugging his milk.

Ugh. That was on my schedule for tomorrow.

"How'd it go?"

He shook his head in disbelief. "It was unbelievable. She was freaking awesome. By the time I left, I'd learned more with her than in two weeks in the classroom. Sometimes you need something to get over the hump, I guess."

I was *very* happy to hear that.

"That's awesome, man. If I don't get this stats shit figured out, there'll not only be no scholarship for me, there will be no football, period."

Tutoring. Another thing to load on to my already-packed schedule. If only I could give up sleeping.

I shoveled the last of what was on my plate into my mouth and stood. "Gotta get back to work."

We bused our tables and Garrett headed out. On my way back to the kitchen, Atlas called me over.

"Hey, Whitlowe," I said.

"Dude. Could you take my tray, too?"

He held it out, while pressing his lips together to keep from laughing.

He was lucky I didn't smash him in the face with it. In my old life, that's how problems like him were dealt with.

"Suck my dick, Whitlowe," I said and continued on my way, his friends hooting and hollering.

What a waste of fucking flesh.

I had half a mind to tell him I'd earned my spot on the team, rather than inherited it as part of a money-making legacy.

But I kept my mouth shut.

He should learn to do the same.

8

ZANE

Whoa.

Garrett hadn't told me our stats tutor was so cute.

I extended my hand. "Hi. I'm Zane Rafferty. Most people just call me Z, though."

"I'm Franki. Most people just call me Franki," she said with a smile.

Okay. She had a sense of humor.

I grabbed a seat opposite her in one of the tutoring center's study rooms and was pleased to see that closer up, she was even prettier. "I'm sorry I'm late." I dug through my pack for my notebook. "According to my coach, I haven't mastered the fine art of time management. At least not as well as I need to."

That was an understatement.

"What's your schedule like? Do you practice every day?" she asked.

Fuck. Where to begin.

"During the season we have strength training from six a.m. to eight a.m. Then the team has a short meeting and we have our classes between nine a.m. and two."

Her eyes widened. "Well, what if you have a class that doesn't fit. Between nine and two?"

Cripes. She wasn't just cute. She was actually beautiful with her chin-length glossy black hair, porcelain skin, and bright red lips.

My kind of woman. I wasn't into the preppy sorority girl type. Given where I'd come from, they were too sheltered for me, and we ended up having little in common. Besides, not many of them wanted to be with a former gang member, not that I shared that freely.

She was about to find out about the crazy life of a college athlete. It was always a shock the first time I told anyone.

Hell, it shocked me when I first learned how outrageous our schedules were.

"If your class doesn't fit into that time slot, you don't take it. One of my teammates wanted to major in engineering, but the classes started too early and interfered with morning training. He had to switch majors."

She reacted about the way I'd expected her to—with disbelief.

"I know," I said. "Student athletes—well, depending on your sport—are, in a sense, employees of the university." I laughed. "We don't have the same flexibility that you do in pursuing our education."

It was a strange existence. You had to either be in love with the sport you were playing, really need scholarship money, or both, in order to pull it off. Any less than a one hundred and ten percent commitment would show right away. The pace was brutal.

"So, after classes we go to the training center and watch tapes from the prior day where the coaches give us tips and ways to improve. Then we're on the field practicing until six pm. After that we shower, eat dinner, have a final brief meeting for the day, do homework and study, then get to bed.

For a moment, her mouth dropped open. Then she composed herself. "That is... insane. Why do you do it?"

Good question. "The guys do it for a variety of reasons, but I do it for the scholarship. Plain and simple. Except I don't have a scholarship right now. Hoping for one for next year though. So on top of everything else, I have a part-time job in the athletes' dining hall."

I was one of the very few players who worked during the semester. Coach tried to discourage it, but if you needed to make money, you needed to make money.

Her eyes bugged. "Holy crap. That doesn't leave much time for studying."

I nodded. "And thus why I need help in stats. I'm okay in my other classes, English and history, because I enjoy them. But stats is a different sort of beast."

She laughed a lovely sound that I wouldn't have minded hearing on a regular basis. She reached to pat my hand. "Let's get going then. Hopefully, we can help you master this so you have one less thing to worry about."

Well then. Maybe tutoring wasn't going to be so bad.

"You know, you seem familiar," I said. Was it possible we'd met?

She blushed a little and tilted her head. "Really?"

"Yeah. Do you ever watch our practices? Or come around the training center?"

She looked at me like I'd asked whether the world was flat. "Oh no. Sports aren't my thing."

"You don't like sports? Like at all?" I asked.

She pressed her lips together and thought before she answered. "Not really. I mean, I like watching the Olympics sometimes. Depending on the sport. You know, figure skating. Gymnastics. Stuff like that."

I'd be damned.

"Have you ever been to a football game?"

She shook her head *no*. I couldn't tell whether she was embarrassed or proud.

Okay. She'd just delivered me a big challenge. One I was happy to take on.

"I bet you'd have fun if you came to a game with me. I'd show you how exciting they are."

She laughed. "Yeah, but you can't because you're down on the field playing."

I laughed. "You got me there."

I pulled my phone out of my backpack. The damn thing had been vibrating nearly the entire time I'd been with Franki.

Shit.

It was my little sister.

And she never called.

9

FRANKI

"I gotta take this call."

His face stricken with alarm, Zane jumped up and walked to the corner of our meeting room.

I started looking over his stats homework.

I didn't want to eavesdrop, but we were together in a room not much bigger than a closet.

"Lilly. Lilly, slow down," he said quietly, glancing over at me.

I flipped through the pages of his stats book while sneaking discreet glances.

He wasn't what I'd expected. Where Garrett was

clean cut, Zane was more street smart with his craggy complexion and a scar under his eye.

And his eye contact was incredible. Unnerving, really.

He scraped his fingers through his hair, giving me a peek of a tattoo that started at his wrist. "Okay, sweetie, just tell me what happened," he said.

I had no idea who he was talking to, but there was clearly some sort of crisis going on that was causing him pain. His huge body was hunched over, with his free hand over his eyes, like if he couldn't see what was going on, then it might not exist.

"No. Wait. Dad did *what*?"

He started to pace.

Good lord. What was going on at the Rafferty homestead? And who was Lilly? Did he have a kid?

"Okay, okay," he said, his eyes squeezed shut, "grab James and get in your room. Lock the door. I'll call you later, okay? And stop crying, sweetie."

Whatever was going on didn't sound good.

He lowered his voice. "I love you, too. I'm glad you called. Always call me when you need something."

He ended his call and returned to his seat, shoulders slumped, looking years older than his sophomore status, and like he needed to sleep for a week. Geez, this guy had some serious grown-up problems going on.

"Sorry about that." He looked at his watch. "That

just sucked up about fifteen minutes of our session." He laughed dryly.

This guy was at the end of his tether.

"Is everything okay?" I asked.

"That was my little sister. I'm the big brother and the one she and my little brother turn to."

Holy crap. My heart broke for this guy, and especially for his younger siblings and whatever they were going through.

"I'm so sorry. You have… a lot going on."

He looked at me with defeated eyes.

"I… I can stay later if that would help," I offered.

"I can't. I gotta get to practice," he said wearily.

"What about tomorrow then? We can meet again when you're in a better… frame of mind."

At my understanding words, he dropped his head in his hands.

I was tempted to reach out and offer comfort. But I'd only just met the guy. And now I felt kind of shitty for all my snotty prejudgment.

He sighed deeply. "I have a younger sister and brother at home, and my dad… drinks a lot. I guess he and my mom were getting into it, and it scared the shit out of the younger kids. I'm sorry you had to hear that."

Good lord. And I thought I had problems.

My concerns were so petty compared to his.

"It must be hard to be away," I said.

"You've got that right. When I was home, I took

care of my siblings. Now that I'm not there, well, things are a mess. I should have just stayed at home..." He trailed off.

"What about your own plans?" I asked, sensing a familiar theme.

Sometimes your family thwarts your dreams, and all you could do was keep moving forward.

"I'm the first in my family to go to college," he said. "So, I'm trying to stick to my plans. Some days it's not so easy. Know what I mean?"

Damn. I was surprised to find I had something in common with a college football player. But goes to show that everyone has their challenges. And now that I knew a little background about Zane, I was extra motivated to help him succeed. He deserved it.

And it dawned on me that maybe my own situation wasn't as bad as I'd allowed myself to believe it was.

I flipped through his text book, looking for a place to start where we could have a quick success, so he could walk away feeling like he'd learned something, when I heard a little snore come from his direction.

I looked up to find he'd dozed off.

Wow.

I'd normally be annoyed out of my mind, but this poor guy, burning the candle on both ends needed a damn break.

There were thirty minutes left in our session. Should I just let him sleep?

Just when I was considering what to do, his eyes flew open.

He looked around, momentarily confused. "Shit. I'm so sorry. First I arrive late, then I get a crazy call from home, and then I doze off in your face. I'm just a big old winner, aren't I?"

Wow. I'd never expected a jock to have a sense of humor or be so self-deprecating.

I laughed. "Don't worry about it. Look, let's go over a couple problems, then we'll continue tomorrow."

We worked through several pages in the textbook and without any prompting, he completed a sample problem perfectly.

"And you need a tutor… why?" I asked, smiling.

"I need to get a better grade. I want to be a doctor, so I have to keep my grades up in all classes."

This guy was no slouch.

"You see, I can get a high C, low B without studying at all. I want to get an A."

I just stared at him.

"You can do that without studying?"

He nodded slowly. "I… do very little studying. I have no time to."

"Okay then. Let's get you an A."

10

FRANKI

"Are you ready to go?" Maddy stood with her hands on her hips, tapping her toe.

"Do I have to?" I whined.

She held her hand out to hoist me from a comfy position on my bed, where I was desperate to catch up on the reading I normally would have done during the time I was now spending tutoring.

"Oh c'mon. Please," she begged.

"But you go to auditions all the time. Why is this one different?" I asked, letting her pull me to my feet.

Of course I was going with her to offer moral support. We were still getting to know each other, and

I was glad to do her a favor. I just felt that I needed to protest a small amount.

"It's freaking *Pride and Prejudice*," she wailed.

I got what she was saying. We were both massive fans of Jane Austen, and it seemed only right to treat her work with all the reverence it deserved. And I hadn't been to a drama audition since high school. I was curious to see how they were held in college.

I sighed and reached for a sweatshirt with my free hand. "You can let go now. I said I was going."

Clapping, she jumped up and down, and we headed for the campus performing arts center.

Maddy and I were different from each other in most every way. She was small and blonde, and her parents had a lot of money.

I was tall with black hair, and my parents were broke.

But what we did share was having been drama nerds in high school. I'd left those days behind, however regretfully, because my parents had insisted it was a waste of time and that I wouldn't have time for clubs and such in college. But Maddy still clung to the hope that she'd someday get a lead in a play, and even more importantly, one in something like a production of *Pride and Prejudice*.

Once we were backstage, Maddy began to chatter.

"Oh my god, oh my god, oh my god. I'm so nervous," she whispered.

Personally, I thought if she were that nervous, maybe theater was not for her.

I patted her on the back. "You rehearsed the hell out of this. You're going to kill it," I offered.

Finally, she was called.

She walked onstage and found her mark, indicated by two crossed pieces of tape. Before she started speaking the lines I'd helped her with so many times that I could probably recite them myself, she glanced my way, where I stood in the wings. I gave her a thumbs up, and she turned to face the artistic director and his team.

"Hello, I am Maddy Browne, and I'm auditioning for the role of Elizabeth Bennett."

From the wings, I took one step onto the stage to better hear her.

The guy in charge nodded politely. "Thank you for coming, Maddy. Please dive in whenever you're ready."

Maddy closed her eyes while she stretched her neck. Then, she aimed her gaze toward the theater's empty seats, and started her monologue in a crisp, clear voice.

While she spoke, the director and his team looked at each other, nodding.

How cool. Maybe she'd get the part.

But when she finished and said thank you, the director stood and pointed at me.

Me.

Crap. I probably shouldn't have been standing on the stage. I took two steps back to get out of view while I waited for Maddy. I wanted to get the hell out of there before someone scolded me.

I was just not in the mood.

But that's not how things went down.

"Miss? Oh, miss? You with the dark hair?" the director called.

Shit. He was talking to *me*.

Here came the reprimand.

"Miss?" he called again.

I peeked my head around the corner. "Yes?" I said quietly.

"Can you come out where we can see you, please?"

Jesus. What were they going to do? Crucify me?

He looked me up and down, and then turned back to his team, who nodded at him.

What the hell was going on? I stole a glance at Maddy, who was as confused as I was.

"What's your name?" he asked.

"Franki. Franki Crawford."

"Do you have any acting experience, Franki?" he asked.

What?

"Um, yeah. I mean, yes. I was in drama in high school. I starred in Grease."

He turned to look at his buddies again, who nodded back at him with approval.

"Would you read for this role, then? I know you're not prepared, but just take these pages here and read them for us if you would." He waved Maddy off the stage.

"Um, well, I'm not auditioning. I just came with my friend here," I said, pointing.

Maddy looked at me, then back at the director, nodding in agreement.

He smiled patiently. "We… we were thinking you had the look we were going for—"

"For Elizabeth Bennett?" I interrupted, incredulous.

I couldn't help it. I probably looked the least Elizabeth Bennett-like out of all the Elizabeth Bennett wannabees in the universe.

The director laughed. "We're approaching this play a little differently than it traditionally has been. We want to modernize it. And a modern Lizzie would be a strong, kick-ass woman who looks something like you. So if you'd like to read, we'd love for you to. If not, that's fine."

Me? Read?

I *guess* I could.

I tentatively walked out on stage and took the sheets of paper the director held out to me. I looked over the section he'd highlighted, and skimmed it quickly.

It was funny. I hadn't auditioned for a play in a long

time but holding a script and standing onstage felt so familiar.

Comfortable, actually. And good.

Really good.

I cleared my throat and started to speak.

I wasn't aware of where Maddy was, or even the director and his posse. Hell, at that moment, I couldn't even have told you what year it was. All I knew was that I was Jane Austen's beloved Lizzie, with her stubborn ideas about love and the way the world worked.

And it was freaking awesome.

The director smiled when I finished. "Thank you, Franki. We appreciate it. We know it's not easy to audition cold."

I figured that was my hint to leave, so I went backstage, where I found Maddy fuming. The hate in her eyes sent serious shivers up my spine.

"Don't be upset, Maddy. Nothing will come of it," I said, waving off her concerns.

Great. Now she was going to be pissy.

Maybe even more than pissy,

She took a step toward me, and I backed up. Good lord, she was really bent out of shape. It's not like I was trying to steal her damn part or something.

"You could have said no," she spat. "But don't worry. You sucked, anyway."

She turned on her heel and stormed off.

While that was a shitty thing to say, I knew she was

right. I was way out of practice, and was surprised the director and his cronies didn't shut me down before I'd even finished.

And now Maddy was livid.

Ugh. I hadn't wanted to come to begin with. That's what I get for doing someone a favor.

On my way back to the dorm, since Maddy had deserted me, I stopped by the dining hall for a sandwich to bring home so I could finally dive into studying. But before I could, my phone vibrated.

"How's it hanging, girl?" Daniel sang from his car microphone.

I'd know that tinny sound anywhere. He'd bought the cheapest mic available.

"Daniel, is there anyone in your car with you?"

I didn't need any more of his Uber passengers to hear my personal business.

He sighed. "No, girl. Nobody. I gotta get a couple more fares and I'm eligible for this month's bonus pool."

"That's incredible. You're really making this Uber thing work."

He loved the flexibility, not to mention the opportunity to meet new… friends.

"Oooh. I just got another fare. Now tell me real quick what the football players are like, and please tell me big and stupid because that's just how I like them."

I sat on the dining hall steps and unwrapped my

sandwich. I was starving and remembered I'd missed lunch.

"They're big, Daniel. But they're not stupid. Sorry to burst your bubble."

"Eh. No matter. Now, when can I meet some of your new friends?" he asked.

"You can meet them anytime you want, but I don't think they play for your team. So to speak," I said.

"Oh, honey, you'd be amazed how many butch athletes just love to suck—"

"Hey, Dan, I gotta go. I'll call you later."

I didn't want to picture either Garrett or Zane sucking anything. I just wanted to teach them stats and collect my paycheck.

And maybe enjoy looking at them for as long as our tutoring relationship lasted.

11

ATLAS WHITLOWE

"Get off my fucking car."

I hovered over two punk-ass fraternity bros trying to steal my license plate. As expected, when they realized they'd been busted by none other than *me*, sheer terror splashed across their faces.

Busted.

"Get the hell out of here," I said, gesturing with my chin. "You're lucky I don't beat the shit out of you."

They rose from their crouched positions in front of my SUV's license plate, which read STATEQB, guilty screwdrivers in their hands. And even when fully standing, they still had to crane their necks to look up at me.

One of them extended his hand, as if I might want his screwdriver. "Um… look… it was a dare. We're frat pledges and they told us—"

I bent down to get in their faces. "I said get out of here before I lose my temper."

They glanced at each other, then at me, and ran like hell, looking back over their shoulders once to make sure I wasn't following.

That would give them a good story to take back to their damn frat. I could hear it now.

"Dude, we almost got our brains beat in by Atlas Whitlowe…"

Like I would touch their scrawny asses. I just wanted to scare them.

Mission accomplished.

I ran my fingers through the new fade the barber had given me and I climbed into my Toyota 4-Runner, a gift from my dad when I'd made State's football team.

I'd skipped my afternoon psych class to get a haircut and now needed to hustle to the training center to watch yesterday's videos and get taped up for practice. Sometimes cutting class was the only way to get shit done—not optimal, but how the hell else was I supposed to get a haircut?

My routine was grueling, but to be honest, it was pretty much all I'd ever known.

As I steered toward campus parking, a couple cute girls holding their books close stopped on the sidewalk and pointed at my car, then looked up at me and smiled. If I hadn't been in a hurry, I might have stopped to chat them up, but there was no time. I just gave them a friendly wave and drove by. Maybe I'd luck out and meet them another time.

If not, there'd be plenty of other girls. There always were.

I didn't particularly like driving around in a car with vanity plates, especially ones that screamed I was the school's top quarterback. In fact, I thought it was kind of a douche-y move, but my old man had been so freaking excited I made it on to the same team he had, that he expressed himself by dropping a wad of cash on a car and the stupid plates.

I'm not going to lie. It was nice to have a car when I needed one. But I rarely if ever did, so it basically sat in the parking spot Coach had finagled for me, and was a target for dumbass pranksters like the kids I'd just chased off. My plates had already been stolen twice before, and I had no doubt it would happen again. But my dad's secretary took care of getting new ones, just like she took care of just about every other little detail of our lives, so when it came down to it, it was no skin off my back. I just made a phone call and shit was fixed.

Yeah, Dad was all over what he called the 'Whitlowe tradition,' and even more so since I'd gotten a full ride to play ball. The man was loaded but loved getting a deal, and the fact that he didn't have to shell out any money for my college education thrilled him to no end. He was already counting on the day when my kids—his grandkids—followed in our footsteps.

I left the car in the parking spot where it spent most of its time and started hoofing it to the training center. I was cutting it close timewise, and if there was one thing Coach could not tolerate, it was lateness. Especially from me. How many times had he told me that as team quarterback, I was a role model for the other guys? Blah, blah, blah.

I spotted some of the other players heading to the training center, but when I saw our newest guy, Zane Rafferty, I singled him out for a chat.

He was a funny guy, Zane. Serious and hard-working, like he carried the weight of the world on his shoulders. I wasn't sure he had a sense of humor or even much of a personality, that's how much he kept to himself. Who knew, maybe he did. Word had it he was the first in his family to go to college, and he wasn't getting any money from the team yet, thus the shit job he had to take in the dining hall. But he was a damn good football player.

"Yo, Z. How's it going?" I asked, jogging.

He looked back over his shoulder and stopped, waiting for me to catch up. I knew he didn't want to be obviously unfriendly, but the scowl on his face said it all. He hadn't warmed to me yet, and probably just plain didn't like me, but I knew he was a good guy and wanted him to think the same of me.

"Hey," he said in a flat voice, falling into step beside me.

"How do you think the videos will look today? I'm thinking Coach is going to kick my ass for those two interceptions I threw yesterday in practice."

He just shrugged and looked straight ahead.

I put a hand on his shoulder. "Hey, Z. Can I talk to you for a sec?"

He looked at my hand, and the other players filing by watched for a moment, wondering what was happening.

But there was nothing to see. I was going to make sure of that.

I continued before he could brush me off. "Look, I think we haven't gotten off on the right foot. Sometimes I can be a loudmouth and my jokes are at others' expense. I don't want any bad blood between us."

He eyed me suspiciously, the thin scar under his eye twitching. "What do you want from me, Atlas?" he said.

Damn. He was a hard nut to crack.

But I wasn't going to beg.

So I shrugged. "Wanted to make sure we played well together, man. That's all."

He took a deep breath. "I understand you're going to tutoring, like Garrett and me."

Yes. Something we had in common.

"Yeah. I start tomorrow. *Not* looking forward to it."

Least favorite subject *ever*. And I clearly wasn't alone in that.

"How's the tutor? Is he a real numbers nerd?" I laughed.

Zane tilted his head, proving he thought I had a ways to go before he'd see me as a worthwhile human being. "The tutor is a *she*. Franki Crawford. She's awesome. Pretty, too. So try not to be a dick to her."

Ouch.

He continued walking, so I did, too.

"Look, Z, I'm not gonna be a dick, man. Ease up. But that doesn't mean I'm going to do any of the work, either. I fucking hate stats and am doing the bare minimum to pass."

He stopped again and took a step toward me, pointing his finger. "You see Atlas, that's the very definition of being a dick."

I was speechless, something that rarely happened to me. Jesus, this guy really couldn't stand my ass.

"I'll tell you what else," Zane said, taking another step forward until he was uncomfortably in my breathing space, "if you give her a hard time, that will be an issue for me. Which means, it will be an issue for you. You might get away with all sorts of shit around here, but I'm drawing the line on bothering our tutor."

He turned on his heel and left me standing there, overflowing with mad respect for one of the few people in my life who had ever told me off.

12

ATLAS

Just as I'd thought, Coach raked me over the coals that day, throwing at me one of the hardest practices of my life. I was exhausted and could barely move my sore body afterwards, but I was making my way across campus to stats tutoring because god knew, I didn't want to do anything that might piss Zane off.

"Well, look who it is."

I turned toward the female voice that had just called me out, and damn if I wasn't faced with a couple of stunning girls I'd seen around but never met. They were both gorgeous, one a fair-skinned blonde in a mini skirt and the other, brown-skinned with tight black curls and a low-cut T-shirt.

Holy shit. I met women all the time. But not like this.

"Ladies," I said. "Looks like we've got a little salt and pepper going on here."

They looked at each other and giggled.

"People say that all the time," the blonde said.

The brunette sidled up to me and ran a finger down my arm. "Where you off to in such a hurry, *Atlas*?"

Ugh. I wanted to say nowhere and drag them back to my dorm room without delay. But today was not the day for that.

"I'm off to… a class," I lied.

The entire campus did not have to know I was in tutoring, for Christ's sake.

The blonde moved to my other side, stroking my opposite arm. "We just thought… you might like to take us out for a drink."

I politely slipped out of their grasp. "Like right now? Don't you have classes to get to?"

They looked at each other again and then back at me, smiling. "Sure, we have classes. But we thought it would be a lot more fun to hang out with you."

Once again, I untangled myself. "Sorry, ladies. Can't make that work. But thanks for asking." I continued on my way before poor judgment got the better of me.

As I walked away, I glanced over my shoulder one last time and found them pouting at my rejection. It was crazy how aggro women got when you were an athlete. My dad had warned me, explaining it was a status thing, and he'd been right. These women, the ones who threw themselves at me on a regular basis, didn't actually give a shit about *me*. They just saw a star quarterback on whose arm they thought they might look good.

No ring, no strings, and never without a condom…

Some of Dad's famous last words.

I was actually relieved to arrive at the tutoring center. Which wasn't like me at all. Some skinny guy directed me to a room where the cutest brunette sat waiting for me.

"You must be Atlas," she said, extending her hand.

Wow. Zane hadn't been kidding. The new tutor was beautiful. Not in the way most guys would describe, but she had a *look*.

And that look told me in an instant, among a few other things, that this woman took no shit.

I liked her already.

Or I liked the challenge she was sure to pose.

"I am Atlas, indeed," I said, taking her hand.

"I'm Franki. Franki Crawford."

I crammed my legs under the too-short table we were to share and nodded. "I know. And I hear you're very good, Miss Crawford."

She looked away, and I could swear even blushed a little.

This was going to be fun.

"Atlas, I wanted to start by sharing the note sent over by your coach."

Okay, maybe this wasn't going to be fun.

CAMPUS TUTORING CENTER:

One of my players will be seeking tutoring services from you in the coming weeks. He is the team's starting quarter-back, but he is also marginally committed to academics. Should you have any issues with him not showing up, not doing the work, or being otherwise difficult, please contact me as soon as you can—"

STUFFING my clenched fists under the table and out of sight, I took a deep breath to control the anger—and if I were to be honest, humiliation—surging through me.

Without reading the rest of the note, I tossed it on the table. Coach's concerns were not off base, but I didn't appreciate him giving people a 'head's up' about anything having to do with me. Now this woman's opinion about me was skewed and there was no way we'd start off on the right foot.

I'd have to figure out a way to let him know that his outreach, while well-intended, was overkill.

And I'd have to find a way to win over Miss Crawford. She was the key to my passing stats, keeping my GPA up, and staying on the team.

Not to mention, keeping my father happy.

"Coach can be a little… overbearing."

She nodded, avoiding my gaze. I had to hand it to her. She was nearly as embarrassed as I was by the tone of the letter.

"Shall we get started?" she asked.

"Yup. Let me have it."

13

FRANKI

"HEY, Z. WHAT ARE YOU DOING HERE?"

Atlas had glanced up from his textbook, where we were making painfully little progress, to find Zane standing in the doorway of our little study room.

"Zane," I said, scrolling through my calendar. "We don't meet today. Did you get your dates mixed up?"

But he didn't answer me. In fact, he didn't even look at me. Instead, unless I was seeing things, he glowered at Atlas.

What the hell? I thought they were teammates and all that.

His sudden appearance aside, it was something

looking at the two of them. Being in the sudden company of not one but two oversized humans made me feel very small.

And for some reason, very sexy, too.

Seriously. I wasn't petite by any means, but I think each of these guys was at least two heads taller than me. Their shoulders were pure mounds of muscle, so sprawling I couldn't imagine where they got their clothes, and their hands positively dwarfed mine.

In short, they were freaks of nature. Monsters, really, but in a good way. And also, quite handsome.

Atlas leaned back in his chair, his face covered in surprise. "Dude, guess you're really loving stats, coming here when you didn't have to," he joked.

Zane didn't smile. Instead, he headed straight for Atlas. "So, are you doing your work? Or fucking around?"

Eyes wide, Atlas put his hands up. "Look buddy, we're studying here. If you have an issue, we can talk it out later."

Zane stared Atlas down. "Just wanted to make sure you remembered our earlier conversation."

Earlier conversation?

What the hell were they up to?

I started to stand, wondering if I were capable of stopping a fight before it started—because I knew there was no way I could stop it *after* it started. "Um, guys, is there something going on I need to know about—"

Their heads snapped in my direction and just as quickly back toward each other, like two big cats facing off.

Okay. These guys had some sort of beef. That much was clear. I didn't know what it was, nor did I really care. When it came down to it, I didn't even care whether they passed stats except for how it might reflect on me and the tutoring center. If they weren't committed enough to put in the work, well, they deserved to fail. If they lost their spots on the football team, so be it. I wasn't sweating over their choices.

Particularly Atlas's. I knew Zane had a lot of shit going on, so I could almost excuse him, but from the moment Atlas had arrived, he'd been joking around, wanting to do anything other than learn the concepts I was trying to get him to absorb.

He'd assumed I cared about sports like all these jocks did. Seriously, they were so surrounded by sports fanatics they were oblivious to the fact that there were other ways to spend one's time.

Hey how about some exposure to the theater, guys? Bust out, try something new, why don't you?

But I had to give him credit for being true to himself. He didn't like this subject—maybe he didn't like any of his subjects—and he wasn't about to pretend that he did.

Before we'd even gotten started, he was trying to

make me his friend. It was cute and annoying at the same time.

"Hey, you like football?" he'd asked. "Let me get you some tickets sometime. And not the shitty seats in the student section."

Here we go again. Is that what these guys did, tried to impress people with their stupid free tickets? And did it work? Did girls just fall at their feet for the honor of sitting on an uncomfortable bench in the blinding sun to watch them pummel each other worse than Roman gladiators?

I just didn't get the appeal.

While they continued bickering, I considered walking out. I didn't need to get sucked into their drama. But I remembered how I got paid relatively well for tutoring these Neanderthals. Some shit came with every job, and maybe this was just par for the course— the extra garbage I had to put up with for my extra pay.

I thought of my brother and sister, both now safely ensconced in their first after-college jobs. They'd sailed through the fancy private universities my parents had shelled out the money for without a concern.

No part-time jobs for them.

Not that I was bitter.

Yeah, right.

And there I was, stuck at State. With two bickering football players wasting my time.

"Z, would you relax? Franki and I are trying to

make progress on this stuff," Atlas said, confused about Zane's aggression.

Making progress? I'd call that a little optimistic. But I kept my thoughts to myself. I was not getting involved.

Regardless of how hot these guys were.

"Hey, Atlas and I have only ten minutes left. I'd like to get back to our work if you don't mind Zane."

He glared at Atlas one last time and headed for the door, his face softening when he turned to me. "Sounds good, Franki. Just keeping my friend here on the straight and narrow. Making sure he wasn't wasting your time."

That's what this was about?

Zane felt like he had to *protect* me or something? Damn. I sure as shit hadn't seen that coming.

"See you tomorrow, Zane," I chirped, hoping to hurry him out the door before he exploded.

I turned back to Atlas. "So. Where were we?"

14

FRANKI

"Why are you practically running? I can't keep up."

Maddy, who'd been two steps ahead of me since we'd left the dorm, turned around and rolled her eyes. "You're such a slow poke. C'mon. You know I'm in a hurry."

Her initial anger at my trying out for what she considered *her* role in *Pride and Prejudice* had dissolved as soon as she'd convinced herself she was sure to get the part herself, and that my auditioning was some weird, insignificant fluke. We were back on friendly terms, however tenuous, and she'd begged me to accompany her to check the audition results.

Already congratulating herself, she was grinning ear to ear, walking with her head up and shoulders back like she'd won an Academy Award.

Catching my breath, I followed Maddy through the building's labyrinth of halls to the director's office, where a large crowd was gathered. Everyone craned their necks to read the notice hanging on the bulletin board just outside his door.

To Maddy, it was the most important thing she'd read all semester.

"Shit. Everybody's already here," she whined like she was the only one interested in knowing if she'd won her role.

She was certain she was a shoo-in. Even though the auditions were over, she'd continued practicing the part's lines and her parents had even sent her a gift in anticipation of her assured good news.

I'd watched her gleefully open a box of new clothes, mostly consisting of expensive cashmere sweaters, while I pulled on another hole-y sweatshirt.

I had my fingers crossed for her. I really did.

I leaned against the wall to stay out of the way while Maddy pushed to the front of the crowd. I was surrounded by a swirl of hoots and hollers, presumably of the folks who'd gotten good news about the parts they wanted, and people slinking away with slumped shoulders and drooping heads who'd gotten bad news.

Theater could be a bitch that way, I knew from experience.

Which was Maddy going to be? Hooting and hollering I hoped, for her sake.

But that's not exactly how it went down.

I looked at the crowd around me, thinking about the life of college theater nerds and wondering if I were missing out. I'd loved the camaraderie of the drama group in high school, goofball outcasts that we were.

I'd even considered majoring in theater for about five minutes before my parents convinced me I'd go nowhere with it and needed to prepare for a profession that paid well.

So, I'd chosen to major in psychology. I'd be a therapist. While I might not have the passion for it that some of my classmates did, I enjoyed my coursework and figured I had some good job opportunities in my future.

Maddy pushed her way back through the crowd, marching right up to me, wearing an expression I'd never seen on her before.

"How'd it go?" I asked hopefully.

She sneered. "Why don't you go up there and see for yourself?" she hissed.

Then she turned on her heel and left me.

What the fuck.

Since the crowd had mostly dissipated, I decided to

look at the casting roster myself, to see what had made her mood turn so suddenly.

I figured she hadn't gotten the part. That much was clear, because if she had, I was sure she'd be screaming loudly enough for the entire campus to hear. But because she hadn't given me a straight answer, I figured that since I was there I might as well see for myself.

I approached the bulletin board, rubbing shoulders with the last few people who'd come to see the audition results, when I confirmed that, as suspected, Maddy had *not* gotten the role of Elizabeth Bennett.

Instead, *I* had.

I DIALED Daniel the moment I got out of the building.

"You won't believe this," I huffed, trying not to hyperventilate.

"What's up, buttercup?" he sang. "I'm driving a pregnant lady to the hospital right now." His voice wandered away from his mic, and I imagined him looking over his shoulder. "Don't worry, honey, we're almost there."

Good god. I guess when you were an Uber driver you never knew what you were going to get.

"You're really taking a woman to have a baby?"

He lowered his voice. "Yeah. And you should see

her. The contractions must hurt like a bitch because she's making these faces—"

"Daniel, I have a bit of a crisis going on," I interrupted.

He gasped. "Oh my god. What? Do I need to pull over for this one?"

Jesus. Maybe *he* was the one who should be in the drama department.

"No, Daniel, you need to get that lady to the hospital."

He snickered. "I was just kidding, dummy. So what's up? You fuck them football players yet?"

"Daniel, don't talk like that when you have people in the car," I hissed.

He laughed. "Don't worry. She can't hear. She's moaning like she's going to die."

Good lord.

"Okay. Whatever. Listen to this. Remember I told you I went to the *Pride and Prejudice* auditions with my roommate Maddy? Just to offer moral support?"

I heard his car screech to a stop.

"Here you go, honey. Good luck!" he called.

A door slammed in the background.

"Whew," he breathed. "If she had her baby in my back seat, I was going to be pissed. Blood and guts are so hard to get out of upholstery."

I didn't know how he knew that, and I didn't want to know.

"Daniel. Focus."

"Right. Right. Continue," he said. "This is the thing where they asked you to read lines, right?

I wandered over to a spot of shade on the grass and sat to calm myself.

"Exactly. So, Maddy didn't get the part. Guess who did?"

A shriek nearly split my eardrums. "No. Fucking. Way."

"I did, Daniel. I actually got the part. And it was a cold read. I wasn't prepared or anything."

I lay back on the grass, hoping that would stop the spinning in my brain, and looked up at the sun peeking through the leaves in the tree above. It was so peaceful. So simple.

Unlike my life.

"Congrats, baby. I'm happy for you. I'll be there on opening night with bells on, sitting in whatever free seats you get me."

"There's more to the story, Daniel."

I didn't know why I should be freaking out. I hadn't done anything wrong.

But Maddy wouldn't see it that way. Sure, we were roommates and did some things together, but she was obviously the type who'd turn on you in an instant if it suited her.

"There's more to the story? Like what?" he asked.

"Okay, so I got the lead role.."

"Yeah, yeah. I got that part. What else?"

I took a deep breath.

"Well, Maddy *did* get a role. She's my understudy."

Daniel sucked in a long, deep breath. "Honey, you need to move out of that dorm, right now. She's gonna try to murder you in your sleep. I saw it in a movie once—"

Oh my god. I didn't need him adding to my momentary anxiety.

"Daniel. Ihavetogo," I blurted, and tapped the call over.

I didn't think Maddy would try to murder me in my sleep, but the rest of the semester was going to be mighty uncomfortable.

15

GARRETT

"Do you mind if we get out of here?"

Franki followed my gaze through the glass walls of our meeting room to see several of the people in the tutoring center staring our way.

Great.

But where else could we go, was the question. College campuses were pretty public. We wouldn't have any more privacy in one of the libraries, or even the classroom buildings.

"Okay, sure," she said, noticing what was bothering me.

I got that the university didn't want students doing

whatever they might do behind closed doors, and therefore had installed glass to close off the tutoring rooms. But damn if it didn't leave you feeling like you were in a fishbowl.

A fishbowl with lots of rubberneckers, in my case.

That was definitely one of the downsides to being a student athlete, especially for a high-profile sport like football. Most students left us alone to do our thing, but there was always a contingent of people obsessed with us, sometimes to the point of being stalkerish. Then there were those who hated jocks and wanted to see us fuck up or do something otherwise stupid and humiliate ourselves.

And there was a table of nosy bodies sitting right outside the room Franki and I were in, taking a bit too much pleasure trying to guess which subject I might be struggling with.

I had an idea. Why not answer their questions? Satisfy their curiosity?

I slammed my textbook closed and held it up for them to see. I pointed at it, then myself and rolled my eyes.

They quickly looked away, embarrassed but smiling.

I turned back to Franki, amused by the exchange. "I know where we could go. Back to my dorm," I suggested.

I'd blurted it out before really thinking, and wasn't

surprised that her eyes widened at my idea. In fact, it was kind of remarkable that she didn't slap me across the face when I thought about it.

I immediately help my hands up like a stop sign. "Wait. Wait, that came out wrong. Shit. I'm sorry."

Dammit. She was going to think I was after a booty call, a repeat performance of our one-nighter from the beginning of the semester.

She sat back in her chair, arms crossed, giving me a world-class stink eye.

I shook my head, feeling like the jerk that I was. "I didn't mean anything funny by it. I just thought no one else would be there. But I totally understand that doesn't work for you. Shit. Sorry. I wasn't really thinking."

Not that I would mind a repeat performance. At all. Franki was sexy as hell, and now that I was getting to know her a little better, I actually found myself looking forward to our tutoring sessions. But in spite of our one night together, she wasn't a booty call kind of girl, and with her thinly veiled dislike of jocks, I doubted she had any intention of hanging out with the likes of me.

It was funny. Some women on campus threw themselves at us guys, and some acted like we had leprosy. There wasn't much in between.

Preconceived notions and all that.

"I... I guess we could go to your dorm."

I liked her hesitation. If I wanted to hang out with her, I had to work for it. Not that I did. I didn't have time to date. And I supposed that's why most of us players just hung out with the women who pursued *us*. There was no time or effort involved—two things in short supply for a guy like me.

"It's five minutes' away," I said, as if she'd never been there.

She shrugged. "Okay. Let's go."

I had another motivation for requesting privacy, and Franki was about to learn what it was.

When we got to the suite I shared with Zane, we set up on the kitchen table.

Franki looked around. "It's funny how different this dorm is. My building has the old-school traditional rooms. No suites with private bathrooms."

I followed her gaze. "I like it. It's awesome to have a kitchen, and in this dorm we only have to share our rooms with one other guy. Some of the suites in the other dorms, they cram four people into."

"Is that because you guys are athletes?" she asked sarcastically.

I nodded. "Yes, it is. The more senior players even have their own rooms. Atlas, for example, is just next door."

"He told you I was tutoring him, too?"

"Yup. Zane as well. He's my roommate, in fact."

Her eyebrows rose. "Oh. Okay. Do you guys ever study together?"

I had to laugh at that. "Are you kidding? That would be like the blind leading the blind, now wouldn't it?"

She opened my book to the place where we'd left off. "Well, hopefully we'll be changing that, right? Now, please read me the first problem."

I took a deep breath. While we'd had a few tutoring sessions together, I'd always managed to get her to read out loud instead of my doing it. But I knew I couldn't put her off forever.

So I dove right in.

"What... are... the... chances... of..."

I kept going, occasionally glancing at Franki to see if she'd figured out what was going on.

The kindness in her eyes let me know that she did.

I grabbed a sip of water when I'd finished reading out loud. I didn't do it often, but when I did, it really dried me out.

"You're dyslexic, aren't you?" she asked.

Busted.

I nodded. "Yup."

She sighed. "Holy crap. That must make school really hard."

She had no idea.

"It does. But I was diagnosed young and was taught how to compensate. So I'm pretty good at hiding it. *Most* of the time."

She tilted her head and a smile grew from her bright red lips. "Until you have to read out loud, right?"

"You got it."

She sat back in her chair, studying me. "Why didn't you tell me from the get-go?"

I looked down at my hands. "Didn't want to. I don't like people to know."

"Do any of your instructors know? What about the coach?"

I shook my head. "Nope. None of them know. I mean, some of them might suspect if they're familiar with it, but those who aren't would probably never know."

"Okay. So let's solve this," she said, picking up a pencil.

"I guess I could do that," I joked.

She laughed. "You better. If you don't do well in your class, I could lose my job."

I threw my hands up. "Okay. But what do I get if I do the problem? Do it perfectly, I mean?"

She raised an eyebrow. "Um, well, I guess you get to pass your class and keep playing football."

It was time to take a chance. Hell, what did I have to lose?

"What else do I get?"

She looked confused. "What else do you want? A lollipop? A cookie?"

My gaze wandered from her eyes to her lips and

back again. "A kiss. Just a kiss," I said, hoping she wouldn't slap me across the face.

But she just rolled her eyes and smiled. "I knew it. *Come back to my room. We'll study!*" she mocked.

Laughing, I held my hands up like a *stop* sign. "Fine. Fine. You got my number."

She smirked. "Let's see how you do the problem first."

Hot damn. Of course I was going to get that problem right because I wanted my damn kiss. As soon as I finished it, I pushed my notebook toward Franki. She looked it over, then looked back at me and smiled.

"Okay. You win. I'm... I'm proud of you."

I stood and helped her to her feet. Then I wove my fingers into her thick black hair and slowly pulled her to me. When our lips met, she sank into me softly, and I remembered why I'd been so turned on by her the time before.

And why I'd been kicking myself for not getting her phone number to see her again.

But I had my second chance now. And I wasn't letting it slip through my fingers.

THANK god the day's team practice had been mainly running because my shoulder still hurt like hell. In addition, track time gave me the chance to clear my mind. Stats was not the kind of thing I wanted swimming around in my brain.

I'd rather be thinking of the lovely Franki Crawford and the kiss she'd just given me.

As I smiled, remembering her lips, I was interrupted by one of the other defensive ends, who caught up with me on the track.

"Hey," I said.

"Dude. Heard you're in tutoring. Also heard your tutor was fucking hot."

I stepped up my pace. I really just wanted a few minutes to myself.

And I didn't feel like listening to some jack-off talk trash about Franki.

I dug how she was so different from the other girls who threw themselves at football players. Of course, a lot of the guys loved that, and if I said I hadn't enjoyed it on many an occasion, I'd be lying. But to meet someone who saw me as me—and not a football player or anything else—felt damn good.

I guess you could call it validating.

I wasn't an athlete to her. I was just a guy who used to suck at stats, but who was now going to ace the class.

Unfortunately, my teammate, wanting to know about the hot girl, tried again.

"So Garrett, you gonna fuck her?" he asked.

I ran faster. And he did, too.

"C'mon dude, give me some dirt. Or did you already fuck her?"

Okay. That was enough. Something in me snapped.

I turned and shoved him in the chest. "Back the fuck off, asshole—" I bellowed.

Surprised by my aggression, he came back at me, but by then, two other players were holding each of us back.

I heard a whistle from across the field. Coach had seen us. Dammit.

"You two," he hollered, "get over here."

Well shit. I'd just been doing my laps and that asshole had to ruin it all.

"What are you boneheads up to?" he barked when we'd reached him.

"Nothing, Coach," I said. "It's nothing."

He adjusted his baseball cap and nodded. "Good. That's what I wanted to hear. Now both of you idiots wear your cleats and pads tomorrow. You can beat the shit out of each other then. Got it?"

Great. Getting my pads on would require the use of my sore shoulder.

Shit was closing in. The team would know about my injury, just like Franki had found out about my learning disability.

I wasn't sure which was worse.

16

FRANKI

"WHERE WERE YOU?"

Maddy ambushed me with her snotty tone of voice before I was even all the way in our dorm room.

"I was working, just like I always am from noon to two."

I tossed my books on my bed and was reaching into my closet shelves for my comfy old studying sweats when it occurred to me that maybe I'd head to the library to do some schoolwork. I wasn't up for Maddy's shitty mood and the abuse that was sure to follow.

She was apoplectic I'd gotten the part of Elizabeth

Bennet, and even more so that she had to be my understudy.

I *got* it. I did. She'd had her heart set on the role, and to be beaten out by someone who hadn't intended on auditioning. Then to be assigned that person's under-study added insult to injury.

Hell, I'd be upset too, if I were her.

But—I wouldn't be shitting all over *me*. After all, what had I done?

I hadn't even wanted the damn role.

But now that I had it, I'd be lying if I said I wasn't excited about getting back into drama. It had been my one true love in high school, and I'd reluctantly left it behind, believing it was just 'something I did' to while away the awkward teen years.

So while I felt badly for Maddy, I wasn't taking responsibility for her misery. She had to own that.

Like that would ever happen.

She was mad at the world, and I was an easy target, like the low-hanging fruit on a tree. She could lash out at me with few or no consequences, and damn if she wasn't swinging her hardest.

"I went looking for you at the tutoring center. You weren't there," she said in an accusatory tone.

I took a seat on the edge of my bed, thinking perhaps I could somehow initiate a cease-fire. I racked my brains for something I might have learned in my psych classes about human behavior that I could use, but unfortunately, we'd never covered crazy roommates.

I kept my voice kind and patient, while clenching my fists where she couldn't see them. "Why were you looking for me, Maddy? Did you need something? Are you signing up for tutoring? You aren't taking stats, so I'm not your girl," I said with a laugh to lighten the mood.

Didn't help.

She rolled her eyes and flipped her hair like I'd insulted her. "No, I don't need tutoring," she snapped.

Well. We got that out of the way.

"I… I wanted to meet some of your football players." She sniffed.

Okay. I had something she wanted. I could use this as leverage.

I wasn't surprised. Maddy was, for better or worse, pretty damn transparent. She'd never been wily enough to hide her motivations. It was endearing on one level, but pathetic on the other to see how selfish and immature she was.

"You went to their dorm, didn't you?" she asked.

A quick grinding in my stomach sent up a warning signal like a fourth of July firework. Was I going to regret my decision to accommodate Garrett?

"I did. Football players don't get much privacy, and

everyone was staring. It made my student uncomfortable."

Maddy sneered. "Yeah, sure. Like football players don't like attention."

"Well, they don't when they're being tutored, I can tell you that—"

"Uh-huh," she interrupted. "What else did you do in his room, huh?"

Okay. I could see where she was going with this.

And sure, I'd kissed Garrett, but that was none of her damn business.

Although it did have me second guessing my decision to go to his dorm. Was I going to regret that? Or was it actually nobody's goddamn business?

"Gosh, Franki," she taunted, "I hope your boss at the tutoring center doesn't find out about you."

"Find out what, Maddy? I don't get why you are being such a bitch."

She looked like she'd been slapped across the face.

And I wasn't done. "Why do you have to assume I was doing something inappropriate, especially with some dumb jocks? I'm not their type, anyway. They like the equally stupid kind of girl who wears lip gloss, push-up bras, and long blonde hair."

I yanked my Converse Chucks back on and stuffed a couple books into my backpack. I wasn't hanging around for the kind of abuse Maddy wanted to throw around. I had shit to do.

But just before I stormed out of the room, I turned to look back at her, and saw what I'd done.

There she sat at her desk, in front of her high-end laptop, wearing lip gloss, a push-up bra, and her long blonde hair.

But I didn't give a shit.

FRANKI

"So, Franki, looks like you are working miracles with these football players."

Filling the time with my own studying while I waited for Zane, I looked up at the tutoring center director, Max.

"Really? Where did you get that?" I asked.

He obviously knew something I didn't.

"Their coach checked in with their instructors and they've already seen improvement."

God, those guys were treated like little kids. I wonder if they kept track of when they pooped, too.

"Awesome. Glad to hear that," I said, hoping he'd go away.

I turned back to my book. He'd given me the creeps from day one, with his imperious overlord tendencies. He was running the freaking tutoring center, not the entire university.

Undeterred, he came the rest of the way into the room and sat on the edge of the conference table.

Kind of like we were friends. Which we were not.

"So, Franki, I've been meaning to ask you if you'd like to have coffee some time."

Was he hitting on me?

"Gosh, Max, I'm so busy these days. Not really doing anything outside working and studying. Well, and I got the lead in a play, so that's taking up a lot of my time, too."

I glanced behind him to see if Zane was here yet, but of course he wasn't. He was always late.

Dammit.

But Max only laughed. "Oh. I see. You've got a thing now for football players, huh?"

Oh my god. Was that what people were assuming? I had *not* seen that coming.

How stupid was I?

"Um, no, Max, and I don't appreciate whatever it is you are implying."

He waved away my concerns. "Oh come on. If I've seen it once, I've seen it a hundred times. You girls get your hooks into some student athlete and hate to let go. But I'll let you in on a secret."

He crooked his finger to draw me closer.

Since he was essentially my boss, I inched a little nearer.

"These athletes? They'll be your best friend when they need something from you. But as soon as they don't, *poof*. They disappear."

Why the hell was he telling me this?

"Max, don't assume you know anything about me. This is my job so I can stay in school. Period."

The meeting room door opened and Zane blew in, a flurry of books, papers, sweat, and breathlessness.

Max, who was dwarfed next to him, hopped to his feet. "Okay. I'll leave you guys to it. But hey, before I go, why don't you put your number in my phone here, Franki? You know, so we can get that coffee?"

Zane looked between the two of us while he settled in, mildly curious.

I grabbed Max's phone just to get him out of my hair. I'd deal with his 'coffee date' offer later.

"That guy seems like a douche," Zane said after the door closed.

"Well. Yeah. But he's my boss, so I have to be nice."

He nodded, rubbing his facial scruff. There was just something so down to earth in his eyes, I couldn't believe he was a big-time athlete.

God, that sounded awful. I should be ashamed of

being such a judgmental bitch. But we all carry prejudices, don't we?

Not so different from the character I was playing in *Pride and Prejudice,* I supposed. Elizabeth Bennett walked around with all sorts of preconceived notions that she had to deal with.

Zane exhaled a deep breath. "Wow. What a day. Now that I'm here, I wanted to ask you if we could study at my dorm like you did with Garrett." He gestured outside the glass walls where half the students —and their tutors—were nudging each other and pointing our way.

Really? Didn't these people have better things to do?

"Oh my god. I'm sorry. That is so rude. Yeah, let's get the hell out of here.

I'd never considered what it would be like to be a football star since I was so far out of the sports loop, but I guessed they were like some strange sort of campus royalty, if something as stupid as that actually existed. And from the way both men and women ogled the guys during their tutoring sessions, it seemed pretty obvious that it did.

The moment we were outside, away from one set of prying eyes, we were faced with about five times more, given the number of people buzzing around campus. Zane's tightly wound energy didn't begin to dissipate until we reached the front door of his building. Once we were inside, it was like he could breathe again.

"Those people who stare are so rude. I'd go crazy if I were you," I said.

Zane unlocked the door to the suite he shared with Garret, and I realized the place had been cleaned up. Guess he'd assumed I'd come over.

Did he know I'd kissed Garrett?

Did he know I'd slept with Garrett?

If he did, he wasn't letting on.

"Supposedly you get used to it. I'm kind of new to it all, so it still bugs me, but the other guys say after a while you just don't notice. And then there are the guys who eat it up. I don't imagine I'll ever be one of those."

Yeah, he did not seem like the man whore type.

After we'd done several stats problems, I realized our hour was almost up.

"Gosh, Zane, you're really getting this stuff. You're gonna ace your class."

He smiled broadly, maybe for the first time since I'd known him. "If I do, it's thanks to you."

Maybe it was *somewhat* due to me, but hell, he was the one doing the work and taking the tests. I'd just helped him absorb the material a little better.

But I'd take praise where I could get it. All I had to look forward to was getting back to my roommate, who'd decided she pretty much hated me. Looking at her scowling face was not a pleasant way to live.

Seriously. We usually went to the dining hall together for dinner, and she wouldn't even do that with me anymore, instead choosing to go with some other girls in the dorm.

Whatever.

"That's nice of you to say, Zane. Thank you."

I started gathering my things to leave, but to my surprise, he reached out and took my hand.

"Really, Franki, I can't thank you enough."

And the next thing I knew, his lips were on mine, totally different from but equally delicious as Garrett's from the day before. What was different now, though, was that Zane pulled me to him, burying his fingers in my hair, gently holding my head. He stopped to look at me, then went back to kissing me.

As if he couldn't get enough.

And to be honest, I kind of felt the same way about him.

But it didn't matter. I needed to get out of here. I shouldn't be messing around with either Zane or Garrett. It would lead to nothing but trouble. My enrollment at State was precarious at best due to my financial situation, and I could not afford to mess it up.

I pulled out of Zane's arms. "I need to go. Sorry."

"Wait, Franki, I'm sorry if I upset you—"

"You didn't," I interrupted. "I… I… just shouldn't be here, doing this."

I ran for the door and tripped over a chair leg, catching myself before I face-planted, but causing a huge ruckus when the chair crashed to the floor in the process.

I dashed out, and who did I run into on my way but Atlas, just coming in.

His face was covered in surprise. "Hey, Franki, what are you doing here—"

But before he could finish his sentence, I was out the door and running back to my own dorm, where I wasn't sure the situation was going to be much better.

18

ZANE

"Zane, you look a little slow there."

In the dimly-lit training room, all eyes turned in my direction as Coach assessed a video of our practice from a few days before.

But I hadn't heard a word he'd said.

He pointed at me. "Earth to Zane. You're not gonna get to the playoffs by daydreaming."

I snapped to. "Sorry, Coach."

He replayed the clip, and this time I studied it, watching how I'd nearly missed a hand-off from the quarterback.

He was right. "Yeah. I see it." I nodded.

I didn't add that Atlas was late in the hand-off, which was what had really fucked me up. I didn't throw people under the bus like that.

But I should have anticipated any potential problems. When you played as a team, no one person messes up a play, and no one person gets credit for a play. We had backups for our backups.

Could I have been faster? Hell yeah. A player could always be faster. But I knew my burning the candle on both ends between school, practice, work, and worrying about what the hell was going on at home was taking its toll. I envied my teammates who had nothing to worry about besides freaking showing up.

Satisfied that I'd acknowledged the problem, Coach turned to the running back next to me and began to critique his performance.

I knew I should have been listening. Reviewing practice videos was something that benefitted us all. But my thoughts were stuck on Franki and the kiss I'd given her yesterday.

Just before she'd run out my door like her ass was on fire.

And to make matters worse, while I stood there trying to figure out what the hell I'd done wrong, Atlas stuck his head into my room, the door having been left open as Franki had hightailed it out.

"What did you do? To Franki?"

I was not in the mood.

But when it came down to it, I wasn't sure *what* had happened. I mean, I'd obviously done *something* to piss off or otherwise upset her. Knowing that didn't make me happy. I freaking liked her.

And I wasn't down with Atlas getting in my face. At all.

"Don't worry about it, dude."

He frowned and came into my suite. Without being invited.

"Z, she looked upset."

Oh fuck it.

"We kissed. It was awesome. Then she freaked and ran out."

He looked down at his shoes, then back up at me. "Are you... are you sure she didn't feel, um, forced or something?"

Really? This big-mouth douchebag thought I had to answer to him?

I gathered my things to head to my shift at the dining hall. I sure as hell wasn't going to get any studying done.

"It was consensual if that's what you're asking. Not that it's any of your goddamn business."

He held his hands up like a *stop* sign. "Okay, dude. Take it down a notch. Look, I like her too. I just felt like I should ask. I'm sorry I offended you."

I brushed past him and he followed me out. "I'm heading to work. See you later."

Once I'd reached the dining hall, I pulled on my apron and baseball cap and got to work.

"Z, why are you banging things around so hard? You trying to wake the dead?" Hal asked, frowning at me.

I shook my head. "Sorry, man. Guess I was just letting off some steam."

He walked over to me. "Everything all right? Something up with classes? Or the team?"

I couldn't bring myself to tell him it was about a woman.

I smiled and slapped him on the back. He was a good guy and the last thing I wanted was for him to waste any time worrying about me. He was good to us players and especially me. I think he saw something of himself in me, and that if the world had offered him different opportunities, he might be doing something other than cooking in a college dining hall.

"Hal, it's all good. Just got a lot going on. Know what I mean?" I said with forced cheer.

He looked at me, not believing a word I'd said. "Okay, young man. Keep up the good work."

It wasn't the first time I'd wished my own father were a bit more like Hal.

Instead, Dad was a heavy drinker who bounced around from job to job, barely contributing to the family finances. It was my mom, a nursing assistant, who kept things under control as best she could. But sometimes even her efforts weren't enough, like the day a couple weeks back when my little sister had called me in a panic.

"Hey. Is it your break time yet?"

I looked up from the buffet table I was refilling to see Garrett had just arrived.

I wiped my hands on my apron. "Yeah. Let me go and tell Hal I'm taking my break."

We grabbed our usual table away from the rowdies, and I dove into my bacon cheeseburger. I was freaking starving.

"Dude, why are your eyes so red?" Garrett asked.

I shrugged. "Guess I'm tired."

He shook his head. "Well, you do have a lot going on. Hey, how'd your tutoring session go? In the suite?"

"It was fine until we finished and I kissed Franki. She kissed me back until she freaked and ran out."

His face got serious. "I kissed her the other day, myself."

We stared at each other.

"We both like her then," I said.

I wasn't worried about any conflict between Garrett and me, though. One, we'd never fight over a woman, and two, I had a feeling she didn't want anything to do with us, anyway.

But you never knew.

It was funny Garrett and I both liked her. He was such the all-American guy, and I was kind of gritty and street. I think that's why we'd become such good friends after we'd been matched as roommates.

We saw things in each other that we respected.

And I guess we liked many of the same things in a woman.

"What do you think about combining tutoring sessions? If we're at the same point in the book?" Garrett asked.

It was an interesting idea. It could save Franki some time and maybe we'd get even more done. "I'll text her," I said.

"Cool. Then we can also see if she's interested in either of us, too," he said with a smile.

Or *neither* of us.

Regardless, I wasn't ready to give up.

19

———————

ZANE

"Zane, honey. Is that you?"

I'd set up my grandmother's phone to identify incoming calls, so of course she knew it was me.

But getting her to trust technology was another story.

"Gram. Hi."

I heard a kitchen chair scrape and pictured her in her house shoes and faded apron taking a seat at the kitchen table in order to give me her undivided attention. The multi-tasking of my generation was completely unfamiliar to her. I hoped it always would be.

125

My fractured attention was more often a detriment than not.

"Good to hear your voice, Zane. How's everything going at college?"

She'd been my biggest supporter, scraping together the little money she had to ensure I could get through my sophomore year, my first year at a full-blown university. I owed her everything. Actually, my whole family did, even her son—my father—who sometimes didn't even know what day of the week it was.

"It's good, Gram. I'm busy but I really like it."

Well, I liked it *most* days.

"Honey, if you need money for next year, just let me know. I'll think up something—"

"Gram, no, I'm set for next year. I... um… am getting money for playing football," I lied. I hated being untruthful to my grandmother, but the last thing I wanted was her preoccupied with my college tuition bill.

"Oh, that's marvelous, Zane. I'm glad they're helping you out."

My grandmother knew little about college sports, or even college for that matter, except that it cost a lot of money. In an abstract way, she also knew it was a good thing, and that people with degrees had a big array of career choices, which added a certain level of income security to their lives. But no one in my family had ever gone before, so I was kind of the guinea pig. A controversial guinea pig at that. My father hadn't wanted me to go. My high school coach had. Gram saw to it that I could at least get part of the way through after a year at community college.

Some people work for you, some against you.

If I could make it work, my thinking was, then the same doors might open for my younger brother and sister. Of course, I'd probably be the one to pay for them. But that was fine.

While my thoughts wandered over how I got to where I was, Gram had been prattling on, especially about girls. *Watch out for the girls, especially the ones looking for a meal ticket out of the neighborhood,* she'd always told me.

I wasn't sure why she was so obsessed with the idea of a fellow college student trapping me with her feminine wiles—perhaps she knew something I didn't?—but the number of times she'd repeated her mantra against them was more than I could count.

I'd tried to explain to her that college women were here to make their own way and didn't need to 'trap a guy to get out of the neighborhood,' but it didn't seem to register. So I just agreed with her.

Although from time to time I wondered if she had a point.

In a recent class, a woman who'd always made a point of sitting next to me, flirtatiously offered to let me cheat off her during our next test. I'd thought her offer was strange because one, I didn't need to cheat, and two, who was to say she knew the material any better than I did?

Was she trying to make conversation? Or just generally ingratiate herself?

Bizarre. Some of these college customs were beyond my comprehension.

Even stranger was the guy in my class who'd come up to me after the instructor dismissed us one day.

Apparently, he worked for the university newspaper, a dry, repetitive publication that I flipped through from time to time, looking for something new and un-recycled.

It wasn't that it was poorly written or anything like that, and it was no doubt useful to have something offering all the campus goings-on, but there just wasn't a hell of a lot of news to report on.

Which was probably why the student reporter had approached me.

Turned out he'd learned something about my past.

And he wanted to write about it.

With all the cheer of someone who'd discovered gold, he pitched me his idea. "Zane, I'd like to do a story about you and your former gang life. What do you think?"

Yeah, sure, buddy. I want everyone at State to know about the lowest point in my life and the part of it that one, I wish had never happened, and that two, I'd like to get as far away from as possible. But sure, I'll sit down and talk to you about it.

Was he fucking kidding?

To stall for time, I told the guy I needed to clear it with my coach first.

I actually planned to bring it up with my campus advisor before I even mentioned it to Coach. After all, when Coach suggested I pursue an un-demanding major like physical education rather than my preferred interest in pre-med, I'd felt like I could trust him only to a point.

The only reason he could possibly care what I studied was how much time it did or did not take from football practice, and how much room it took up in my head.

Given the choice, I think he'd like us all to memorize game plays and think of little else.

I liked the man, but after that conversation, I wasn't sure I was up to taking advice on life from him.

But I could think of someone whose input I would like on the proposed newspaper article.

Franki's.

20

FRANKI

I'D KISSED TWO OF THE GUYS WHO WERE MY TUTORING students.

And people said I was a smart girl.

Not so much, I was beginning to think.

I settled into my usual seat in the two-hundred-person lecture hall housing my abnormal psych class and started flipping through my notebook. I was desperate to sort my muddled thoughts and didn't want anyone around me to kick off a conversation about our upcoming test or some other bit of small talk. I needed to disengage my worries and wanted to be ready to learn when I heard a ruckus down below, coming from the first row of the auditorium.

I glanced at the descending seats before me and at first figured the noise was from some pre-class socializing. But then my gaze settled on a small group of outsized humans I recognized as football players.

And right in the middle of them was Atlas.

He was in my abnormal psych class? Why hadn't I ever noticed him before?

Probably because he usually skipped class was my guess.

As female students filtered in, Atlas and his buddies watched, nudging and whispering to each other like a bunch of juvenile idiots.

Nice. Really nice. Next time I saw Atlas I was going to say something to him. It wasn't my business, but I didn't care. It was my classroom too, and I was offended.

In fact, I might even say something to the professor.

But when she finally arrived and started with her lecture, I forgot all about Atlas, and soaked up every word she said.

To my mind, there was nothing more fascinating than unusual human behaviors and thoughts. The class ended before I knew it, and I rushed down the aisle to ask her my questions before too large a crowd collected around her.

But I was interrupted by a tap on my shoulder.

An instant of irritation rushed through me. I really wanted my undistracted moment with my teacher. But I turned around anyway.

Oh.

"Hey, Atlas, I have to talk to the professor really quick—"

He nodded with a friendly smile. "No problem, Franki. Just wanted to say hi. My friends and I were saying earlier how many more women there are than men in this class, and that's probably a good thing for the mental health of this country."

Oh. So maybe he wasn't talking about the pretty girls filtering into the room.

He gestured toward our teacher. "Looks like it's your turn. Better go for it."

I waved goodbye to him and started peppering the teacher with my questions about that day's lecture. But once again, I found my thoughts wandering to the guys I was tutoring, and how they were turning out to be different than I'd thought they would be.

And how my association with them had thrown a wrench into my life in ways I'd never anticipated.

When I returned to my dorm room after my latest tutoring session, I was greeted with the word 'slut' written on a note stuck to my door. To make matters worse, before I could yank it down, some douchebag guy from the next floor up was actually taking a photo of it with his phone.

"Did you put this here?" I asked, elbowing him out of my way.

He looked embarrassed to have been caught recording my shame. "No man. Guys don't do shit like that. We'd just call each other assholes, maybe even fight, and then be done with it. But you girls are serious bitches!" He slunk away, shaking his head.

I tore the note down and hurried into my room, locking the door behind me. Thank god Maddy was out at class because I needed to calm down. If she'd been there, I might have been tempted to smack her across the face, which probably wouldn't have worked out well for anyone.

I suspected she was behind the note on the door since she was still fuming that I'd gotten the role of Elizabeth Bennett. But what managed to surprise me more than her displeasure was how tightly she was hanging on to it.

I mean, what was her exit plan? To torment me until I jumped off a bridge somewhere? Was she really that stupid?

It was all very disappointing and once or twice I wished I'd never read for the part at all.

But most of the time I was thrilled and determined not to let Maddy take away from my excitement about it all. The couple rehearsals the cast had so far—really, just readings sitting around a table—had been freaking amazing. What a joy it was to have something new and exciting to focus on.

But was it worth the harassment? And what if it got worse? Who knew, maybe she had real bunny-boiler tendencies under her perfect long blonde hair and expensive cashmere sweaters.

Thoughts ricocheted around my head until I was dizzy with the inability to make up my mind about the situation.

I shot an email to our resident assistant about getting a new room. Moving dorms was a pretty unlikely thing to pull off mid-semester, but there might be a vacancy somewhere on campus I could take advantage of.

FRANKI

"Hi, honey? How are things?"

Over the phone, my mother took a sip of something, most likely the Diet Coke she drank all day long.

"Mom. I haven't told you I got the lead in a Jane Austen play."

There was silence for a moment. "I thought you were done with theater, Franki. Don't you think this will take an awful lot of time away from your studies?"

So much for a *congrats, good job.*

I'd known a reaction like this might result, but I'd really hoped for some encouragement or praise.

But that was okay. Theater was important to me, not to my mother or family.

"It will be demanding for sure, Mom, but I trust my time management skills. And I'm excited. This is a big part, and I love *Pride and Prejudice*."

She sighed. "Well, it is a great story. I just hope you can juggle the demands of rehearsals with your coursework and job."

"If I do find myself overextended, you can be sure I'll put my classes first."

But I'd be damned if I'd let myself get into a situation like that. I was going to make it all work, whether she thought I could or not.

Finished discussing my life, she turned the conversation to my father's and her plans. "Oh, honey, I think Dad and I have settled on an RV. It's a real beaut…"

She prattled on about their upcoming adventures while I crossed campus to one of my own, which I was definitely not excited about.

Coffee with the director of the tutoring center, Max.

I really didn't want to see him outside work. Not because he was necessarily a bad person, which I suspected he might be, but because I just didn't have time for any extraneous socializing, given my tight schedule. But if circumstances were different, Max was not the kind of guy I saw myself hanging out with, anyway.

I wasn't attracted to guys with more hair than me, or those who weighed less than me—two of Max's distinct characteristics. And to make him even less attractive was how he'd insinuated I might have something going on with the football players I was tutoring.

Which I sort of did, but he had no right to assume that.

Shit. Had I just turned into a huge cliché?

When I got to the off-campus coffee shop, Max was nowhere to be found. I got myself a latte and read the news on my phone while I waited. After ten minutes I was starting to get annoyed that he was late to something he'd been the one to insist on. I finished my coffee and got up from my table to leave when my phone buzzed.

hey franki. where are you?

What? Had I missed him? I looked around the shop again. He wasn't there.

coffee shop.

no way. I'm at the bar next door. I thought we changed it.

No, we didn't change it, and no, I didn't want to go to a bar with him.

I'm heading out, I am pressed for time anyway.

NOOOOOOO! wait right there.

Oh Jesus.

Max came flying into the coffee shop, bursting with a giant smile. "So sorry about the misunderstanding. Just come in for one beer. It will be a quickie."

He grabbed my upper arm and started to pull, but I kept my feet planted in place.

"No, Max, I gotta go. I have a lot to do."

"Oh please," he begged.

Why did he want me to join him so badly?

"Just a quickie," he insisted. "You came all the way down here."

Yeah. No shit.

I looked at his hand on my arm, and he immediately released me.

"Please? Just half a beer?" he pleaded.

Oh for fuck's sake.

"All right. I'll stay for ten minutes. No more."

"Cool," he said gleefully.

I followed him into the dark dive bar I'd been to a handful of times, pausing when I got inside so my eyes could adjust to the dim light. As the outlines of the few people sitting on barstools in the early afternoon took shape, I saw that Max hadn't been sitting alone.

Who was he with?

Max positioned me between him and his friend. "Franki, I'd like you to meet Chuck."

I extended my hand but didn't sit on the barstool they'd pulled out for me. I wouldn't be staying for long.

I turned to Max. "We agreed to meet at a coffee shop. Then, you changed it to a bar and brought a friend. Do you mind telling me what is going on?"

The guys looked at each other, pleased with themselves. "Well, we know that, you know, since—"

He hesitated.

"Since *what*, Max?"

"Well since you're... an open-minded sort of girl, we thought maybe you'd like to... you know... pull a train with us."

I sort of absorbed his words, but they were so outrageous it took a moment longer for them to really sink in, and only a half-moment longer for my anger to follow.

And when it did, it wasn't pretty.

"What did you just say?" I asked.

I'd heard them just fine. But maybe if they repeated their words, they'd realized how fucked up they were.

Silly me.

He mumbled his way through his proposition, the word *train* echoing through my mind.

I took a deep breath to make sure I was still alive, and realized I couldn't see or hear anything around me aside from the fools before me. I also felt that, at least for a moment, I had superhuman strength and if I wanted to, could tear them into smithereens.

But I didn't. I used my words like a real adult. Even though I didn't want to.

"Are you fucking kidding me?" I choked.

Max's eyes widened, and his buddy Chuck scooted back on his barstool.

"Well, Franki, we just thought—"

"You thought *what*?"

Max glanced at his friend, who looked like he wanted to leave. Immediately.

"Well, I thought how you messed around with the football players—"

I got in his face. "You thought wrong, you dumb fuck. Now, don't you ever speak to me again unless it's about the tutoring center, or I will turn you and your sidekick in."

I grabbed the beer sitting on the bar and threw it in his face, then tossed the glass in his friend's direction. He dodged it and it crashed to the floor.

All heads turned in their direction, but I was already halfway out the door.

Why did my association with the guys I was tutoring lead to such bullshit?

And even if I did like them and wanted to mess around with them, why was it anyone's business?

All elbows and ass, I headed back to my dorm room to get some studying in before play rehearsal.

How'd I get to this point? I just wanted to work my way through State, get my degree, and become a therapist.

I hadn't thought that was too much to ask. But shit, maybe it was.

2 2

ATLAS

"Hey guys. You still up?"

I knocked quietly, my ear to the door, in case they weren't.

And lucky for me, the door flew open, and there stood Zane in his boxers and a T-shirt.

"Hey, do you two have a sec?" I asked.

Zane, still not a fan of mine, gestured for me to come in. I joined Garrett in their small living room, where they were watching late night TV before turning in.

"Hey, Atlas, what's up?" Garrett said, clicking the TV off.

"Hi Garrett. I wanted to talk to the two of you with no one else around."

Garrett looked at Zane, who stood stiffly at the edge of the room. "Z, you gonna sit down, or what?" he asked.

He nodded and silently took the seat opposite mine.

I was taking a risk. But I had to do it.

"I'm going to get right to the point. This is about Franki, our tutor."

They glanced at each other before they looked back at me.

I had their attention now.

"I wanted to say that, even though she probably hates me, I've… come to like her. And I wanted to talk about that because I don't think I'm alone in feeling that way."

Without the TV, the room was dead quiet except for the muffled voices coming from the suite next door.

"What makes you say that? About Z and me?" Garrett asked.

I held my hands up as if to say if they wanted me to hit the road, I would. But I hoped they wouldn't.

"Well, I… can tell. First off, she's a cool woman. What guy in their right mind wouldn't be interested? And second, it's obvious to me because of how you talk about her and how you are when you're with her."

I'd watched their tutoring sessions. I couldn't deny

it. I'd stopped by to say hi, and she was busy with them, so I'd hung out.

"Are you here, Atlas, to tell us to back off so you can date her?" Zane asked, one eyebrow raised.

Shit, I still hadn't won over that guy.

"No, Z, not at all. In fact, while this might be a little 'out there,' I was wondering how she'd like to date all three of us. If you guys were down with it, of course."

Garrett leaned forward, resting his elbows on his knees. "You mean, like, we would share her?"

I let that sink in for a moment. "Yeah, more or less. I've… I've done something like this before and it was… awesome."

Garrett sat back in his seat, thinking. Zane remained twisted into a bundle of tension like he normally was. If the guy didn't learn to chill, he'd be dead of a heart attack before he was forty.

But sometimes people surprise you.

"It's… an interesting idea," he said after a moment.

Okay, that was about the last thing I thought I'd hear from Zane's mouth.

We turned to Garrett.

He nodded slowly. "I'm game. 'Course it all depends on what Franki wants."

Damn. I thought they'd either tell me I was crazy, that it was the stupidest idea they'd ever heard, kick me out on my ass, or all three.

But they didn't. Not even Zane.

I stood to go. I'd only wanted to introduce the idea to the guys. The rest would follow.

"Agreed. It all hinges on Franki. Maybe she won't want any of us. If that's the case, then hopefully we can just... be friends."

They looked at me, partially stunned that I'd proposed something so unconventional, and partially relieved that there might be a way to move forward with the girl who was taking up more and more time in our thoughts.

I had one last thing I wanted to say. "Look. I know we haven't been the best of friends. There are some guys on the team who are loud-mouthed douchebags and from time to time I fall in with them. I hope you'll... give me a chance."

I said goodnight and went next door to my room. I needed to think hard about a few things.

I knew I was a privileged fuck. My dad wouldn't let me forget it, along with my obligation to carry on the Whitlowe family name with pride.

I'd had it so much easier than many of the people around me. I didn't have to take shitty part-time jobs during the school year to pay my bills. Hell, my summer jobs were at my dad's company. They worked me hard if for no other reason than to make an example of me. If I weren't related to the old man, none of them would have given me the time of day. I knew it. We all knew it. We just pretended it wasn't the case.

And for the people here at school who assumed I'd made the football team just because my father had played here—well, they could suck it. I didn't become the school's quarterback by sitting around on my ass. I worked for that position. Hard.

And now that I'd accomplished that, I was thinking it might be time to really concentrate on my classes. Smart girls were hot, and I was hoping one smart girl in particular would think I was smart, too.

23

ATLAS

I WAITED FOR FRANKI OUT IN FRONT OF THE GRAD student library, a sleepy building housing publications that were now nearly all available online. Because of that, the place didn't get a lot of visitors and was great to go to when you needed… time alone.

I hoped Franki wouldn't ask how I knew that.

Speaking of the lovely girl, she'd just jogged up the steps in front of me, her short black hair swinging around her face, her Converse Chucks slapping on the old bricks.

"Sorry I'm late. I was studying lines for my play and lost track of time."

Her cheeks were pink and her eyes bright from rushing, and I could hardly stop looking at her.

"Shall we?" I asked, holding the door open as we entered.

She looked around the cavernous first floor doing a three-sixty turn, her eyes wide in wonder. "You know, I think this was one of the original campus buildings. I'm guessing it's a couple hundred years old. Look at the old tile on the ceiling."

I was glad she was enthralled with the building. But I was enthralled with *her*.

In fact, when she was finally done checking out the building and turned back to me, she caught me staring.

"C'mon," I said. "Let's go to the stacks and find a table."

We wandered through the library's ghostly second floor, staffed by a bored librarian paging through a thick novel.

"Let's sit here by the window. It's brighter," she said and plunked down in a chair.

I opened my notebook, moving slowly to stall for time. "Hey, what play are you in?" I asked.

"The drama department is putting on Jane Austen's *Pride and Prejudice*. I have the lead role," she said proudly.

Impressive.

"I can see you as the drama type."

Not that I'd ever known any 'drama types.' But if I had, I bet they'd be like Franki.

"What does that mean?" she asked, smiling.

"Well, you wear black and you're snarky as hell."

Amused surprise splashed across her face. "Me, snarky? Never!"

I raised my eyebrows at her. "When's opening night? I hope I'm in town. I want to come."

The pink in her cheeks spread to the rest of her face.

She was blushing.

And it was goddamn adorable.

"You… you do?"

I slapped my hand on the table to make my point. "Absolutely. I go to the theater with my mother when my dad doesn't feel like going. We always have dinner beforehand. It's a nice mother-son night out."

Franki's mouth dropped open.

"What? You think football players don't appreciate the performing arts? Are you kidding? We're not just Neanderthal meatheads, you know."

Well, some of us were.

I leaned toward her over the desk. "Look, I have something I want to run by you."

She flipped open her own notebook. "Can it wait until we are done? We have a lot to cover today."

"Yeah… it can probably wait. But I don't want it to.

Look, I wanted to tell you that we guys—Garrett, Zane, and myself—like you. Like *want to date you*, like you."

There was no point in beating around the bush. Either she'd be in—or she'd be out.

She pulled her head back and looked at me like I might be crazy. I didn't blame her. I fully expected she'd be thrown for a loop.

Her face got very serious, and she leaned closer. "What… what do you mean?" she asked in a lowered voice.

I got it. Our proposal was… unusual. It would have been strange if she hadn't questioned it.

I looked behind her. "Maybe Zane can help explain."

She whipped around, where he stood right behind her.

"Hey, guys," he said, pulling a chair up to our desk.

Confused, Franki frowned. "Zane. What are you doing here? Your tutoring session is tomorrow."

I was a little surprised he'd shown, too. But I think he was beginning to accept that maybe I wasn't as big an asshole as he'd originally thought I was, and that my idea about dating Franki was an intriguing one.

He made an exaggerated shrug. "Oh, you know. I was just in the neighborhood."

He and I looked at each other and couldn't help but smile.

Franki frowned. "Is this… a set-up?"

Zane tried to stop smiling but was unsuccessful. "Mayyyybe," he drawled.

Franki shook her head. "You guys. What the hell? Atlas, we have problems to practice."

I got up from my chair and Zane followed. "Stats can wait," I said, drilling Franki with my gaze.

She looked back at me, the realization of what was going on clear on her face.

Zane took her hand, helping her from her chair, and they followed me to a long-abandoned office. We went inside, leaving the door slightly ajar.

Hands on hips, she stood across the small room from us, a slow smile taking over her pretty face. "What are you guys up to?" she asked with a laugh.

Zane decided to lay it out. "Franki, both Garrett and I have kissed you. We were thinking it's now Atlas's turn."

Zane, who was demonstrating his new perspective on me, was doing me a solid. I'd have to thank him later.

Actually, he already knew I was grateful.

Franki looked at me, a little confused. I couldn't blame her. How often did a woman come across a group of guys who were cool with something like this?

But I hoped like hell she'd be on board. It was all I could do not to reach out and pull her to me right then. I wanted those lips against mine. And more.

"Of course, Franki," Zane continued, "this is only going to happen if it's okay with you."

A dubious expression crossed her face. "Are you… are you both really okay with this?"

Actually, her expression was more than dubious. She was looking at us like we were out of our minds.

But it was all good. And she was welcome to leave anytime she wanted to. In fact, that's why I'd left the door slightly open—to make it easier in case she was compelled to split.

But she stayed.

With a deep breath, she raised her chin like she was trying to be a badass. "I'd like to kiss you, Atlas. I think that would be… nice," she said.

Oh yeah. She was ready for a little fun.

"Come over here, then."

When she sauntered up to me, I wove my fingers into her hair and gently pulled her to me, our lips meeting for the first time.

And not for the last.

24

FRANKI

HOLYSHITHOLYSHITHOLYSHIT.

I was kissing Atlas, the gorgeous, brown-skinned party boy star quarterback who also happened to be my tutoring student.

With the hunky Zane watching.

I'd have been lying if I said I wasn't turned on as hell.

And what turned me on even more was the softness with which he brushed his lips over mine, and the giant hand nearly encircling my waist as he pulled me close.

I'd never imagined such an oversized human being could be capable of such a gentle touch.

He pulled back, his light brown eyes peering into mine like he was looking for something he'd lost, or maybe something he'd never even had. The corner of his mouth turned up—not quite a smile, but more of a way to let me know he liked where we were at that moment in time.

Zane cleared his throat, and I found him standing immediately to my left.

"You're gonna share, aren't you, Atlas?"

My heart thumped against my chest, and I realized it was a good thing Atlas had a hold on me because my legs were turning into Jell-o.

Two big, hunky men wanted to kiss me? It was both exhilarating and intimidating at the same time. And I was so small in their presence. Cripes, they could have squashed me like a bug if they'd wanted to.

Atlas pressed his lips together in a sly smile, like he was considering Zane's request to share. "I don't know, Z. I kind of like having her in my arms right here."

He shrugged. "That's okay. I can still make my moves."

He gently turned my head toward him and, tilting his own, put his hands on either side of my face and bent to lower his lips to mine.

Atlas loosened his hold on me to give Zane better access, but I was still encased by four arms—big, strong arms—warm and protective and sexy as hell.

I kept one of my own arms around Atlas's neck and

moved another to Zane's. I was so undersized between the two of these guys, it made me dizzy.

While I continued to kiss Zane, Atlas untangled himself from me, and I heard him walk over to the door, which he'd left slightly open. He turned the lock. It was funny, but that little sound took away some of my anxiety and enabled me to throw both my arms around Zane and melt into him.

I'd thought our chaste kiss in his dorm room was nice, but it was nothing compared to the way he moved against me now. And I was grateful he'd never mentioned how I'd run out on him like a freak.

Atlas walked up behind me and with his hands on my hips, ran kisses down the back of my neck and onto my shoulder where he'd eased aside my T-shirt.

Oh. My. God.

I'd never been with two guys and to say the sensation was overwhelming sorely understated it. Simply put, with all the hands and lips on me, I was flying. All my preoccupations with school, work, the play, my crazy roommate, and the ambivalence toward my parents, disappeared. The lightness that followed was a balm—welcome, soft, and relaxing. It gave me room to get out of my head and sink into what the guys were offering me.

Atlas had lifted the bottom edge of my T-shirt and his warm hands were now on my skin, which I hoped he hadn't realized had erupted in goosebumps at his touch. They reached my breasts and pushed aside my bra, and when he gently pulled my nipples, I moaned right into Zane's mouth.

"Z, I think our girl is getting turned on," Atlas murmured.

Zane pulled away to look at me, lifting my T-shirt the rest of the way over my head and dropping it to the floor. Atlas unhooked the back of my bra, and Zane lowered his mouth to one of my breasts.

His rough tongue teased my nipple, sending a shockwave straight to my core. As he did, I dropped my head back into Atlas, who unbuttoned the top of my jeans.

"Let's get you over here," Zane said, guiding me.

He leaned me back on an old wooden desk that had probably seen all kinds of life over the years—but probably nothing like it was about to.

Zane unzipped my jeans and when he started easing them from under my ass, he moaned when he got a load of the lacy black thong I was thanking god I'd put on that morning.

"So pretty, isn't she Atlas?" he said, bending to kiss my tummy.

"Fucking gorgeous," Atlas agreed.

He bent to remove my sneakers, and next thing I knew, my jeans were in a pile on the floor just like my shirt was.

I looked up from my prone position to find Zane

and Atlas admiring me as I lay there for them, and damn if they didn't make me feel beautiful and sexy, and desired.

That's what it was. I felt desired. And powerful. And those sensations turned me drunk with need. If one of the guys didn't start doing something soon, I was going to have to take care of business myself.

But that wasn't a problem.

When Zane had shimmied my thong down my hips and tossed it aside, he pushed one of my legs back and Atlas took the other. I was wide open for them and the exposure was intoxicating and delicious. I wanted them to see me. All of me.

When Zane ran a finger through my slit, I shuddered and arched in reflex.

I wanted them, and I wanted anything they wanted.

"Fucking hot, isn't she?" he murmured.

Atlas agreed with his own grunting approvals, alternating between kissing me and my breasts.

Next I knew, Zane's mouth was on me, his tongue buried between my pussy lips, running from top to bottom and back, tormenting the length of my sex like it was his toy to do with as he wanted.

"That feels so nice," I whispered, grabbing the sides of the old desk for purchase as he circled my clit.

Then he rested a finger at my opening, slowly working its way in. He pulled it out, covered in my juices, and put it to my lips.

"Taste yourself," he demanded.

I greedily took his finger, sucking it hard, enjoying my salty tang. When he pulled his finger back out of my mouth, I dropped my head back and laughed. I couldn't help it.

Crazy. Crazy was what the whole situation was.

And I loved it.

Next, he entered me with two fingers and moved his mouth to my clit at the same time.

I pounded a hand against the desk beneath me, begging for release before I completely lost my mind.

And then it came in waves starting between my legs where Zane's mouth was going to town, radiating across my core and rushing through my limbs like electric jolts. I gasped for air and a throbbing orgasm slammed into me, and didn't let up.

He plunged his fingers into me one last time, going deep, until I thought I would shatter into pieces.

I came again and again, steamrolled by exquisite sensation, as all thoughts left my mind aside from the pleasure engulfing me.

I lost track of the number of times I came. As the aftershocks of my killer orgasm wound down, leaving me limp and raggedy and hungry for a little nap, the guys took turns kissing me.

But I'd lost track of the hour until I spotted an old-school clock on the wall hanging over the door.

Not smart.

"Oh my god. Is that the time?" I asked, bolting up so fast I dizzied myself.

Atlas looked at his watch. "Yeah, it actually is. Funny, because this room probably hasn't been used in years."

"Oh my god." Trying to calm my spinning head, I jumped to my feet, scrambling for my underwear. I pulled on my T-shirt, jeans, and sneakers.

I probably reeked of sex, but there was no time to shower.

"I'm so sorry, but I have to run. I have play rehearsal in five minutes."

Dammit. Atlas and I had done exactly zero stats homework.

I kissed each of their surprised faces, and ran out the door.

FRANKI

"It's my ride or die bitch! How's it hanging, honey?"

Daniel had grabbed my call on the first ring like he always did. Bless him. Best friend a girl could ever hope for.

"Oh my god Daniel. I need your help."

He got silent for a moment. "Are you okay? Did something bad happen? Because if it's that psycho roommate of yours, she doesn't know what crazy-ass behavior is until she meets me—"

"No, Daniel, I'm okay. At least I think I am. And it has nothing to do with Maddy."

He exhaled hard. "Oh. Okay. Because you know I'll fuck that girl up if I have to."

God, I loved him.

But I needed him to listen for once.

"Okay, Daniel," I started, lowering my voice even though I was in my dorm room alone, "I was just with *two guys*."

He shrieked. Not exactly the reaction I'd expected, but okay.

"You. Little. Slut. I love it!" he screamed again.

Shit, I hoped he didn't have anyone in his car. But I wasn't even going to ask. I didn't want to know.

"Was it awesome? Oh, honey, I'm so happy for you. Whew, my girl took a walk on the wild side..." he sang.

"Daniel, would you please *listen*?"

"Oh. Yes. Of course. Continue," he said, all seriousness.

"It's the guys I'm tutoring. They like me. They *all* like me. And they've talked about, you know, dating me. Like all three of them."

He whistled. "Wow. I never knew straight boys would be down with something like that."

"What... what do you mean?"

He sighed impatiently. "Have I taught you nothing? Monogamy is overrated, in my experience. What you're describing sounds like heaven to me."

It sounded like heaven to me, too. But also fraught with all kinds of complications and drama.

"You don't think it's weird?" I asked.

He hemmed for a moment. "Yeah. It is kind of weird for straight people. But I say go for it if you like them. Fuck everybody else."

"Really?"

"Girl, you know how hard it is to find love in this world? Or even *like*? And if you have three nice guys liking you, well, you can't walk away from that. I sure as hell wouldn't."

He had a point.

And yet.

It felt good to know my BFF didn't think I was a freak.

I wasn't sure how other people would take it, though.

A HAND LANDED on my shoulder. Hard.

I whipped around to find Max, about my least favorite person in the world since our run-in at the bar. "What do you want?" I hissed, maneuvering out of his grip.

I knew I was pushing it by talking to my boss like that, but since he'd harassed me, I was pretty much out of fucks to give.

"I wish you hadn't run out on us like you did the other night. It really wasn't necessary," he said.

Was he fucking kidding?

"Max, you obviously have no clue as to the level of insult you dumped on me. But you must have some amount of intelligence, being a college student like everyone else around here. So I'm gonna ask you to put yourself in my shoes. Did you really think I wanted to *pull a train with* you and your buddy?"

People going to and from class filtered around us, and while I had tried to keep my voice low, my comment *pulling a train* caused some turned heads.

And I didn't give a shit.

I started walking, hoping I could lose the idiot.

But, of course, he was right on my heels.

And he grabbed my arm harder this time.

"Max, leave me alone—"

"Hey. You heard her. Get the fuck off," a voice growled from behind me.

Max let go as we turned to see Garrett standing there, his giant hand landing on Max's scrawny shoulder.

Before realizing a man twice his weight was telling him to back off, Max shot him a *who the fuck are you glance*. But when he realized he was outsized by at least two times, *and* that he was facing a student of the tutoring center, he changed his tune.

"Okay buddy," he said like a smart-ass, "hands off. No one's hurt here." He failed to sound like the badass he wanted to be, thanks to his quavering voice.

"She told you to hit the road, dude. I suggest you do that. *Now.*" Garrett stared down at him with such authority, *I* wanted to run away and hide.

Finally accepting he was outmatched, Max took a deep breath and puffed out his chest to save face.

As if.

"Yeah well, I'll be going now. See you guys at the tutoring center."

He strolled off like a man without a care but revealed himself, again, when he glanced back over his shoulder with wide eyes and picked up his pace.

Garrett rolled his eyes and put an arm around my shoulders. "Jesus. What a creep. You okay?"

I nodded. "Yeah. Thank god you came along when you did. He was getting really aggressive, even after I told him *no.*"

He turned to make sure Max had disappeared into the throngs of students hurrying to class and when there was no sign of him, raised the white paper deli bag he'd been holding.

"I got us both smoothies. Maybe this will take your mind off that creep."

He passed me a chilled cup with a straw. Without hesitation, I took a long, delicious draw of fruity slush.

"Oh my god, this is *just* what I need right now. Thank you so much for this, and for chasing off my wannabe stalker. I don't know how I'll repay you."

"Now you're being funny because we both know there are many ways," he said, his eyes twinkling.

26

GARRETT

"I'M SO GLAD TO HAVE THAT OFF MY CHEST."

Franki was one of the very few people I'd shared my learning disability with and because it felt so good to tell her and unburden myself of some of the shame—not all of it, but still—I wondered why I didn't just tell fucking everybody?

I supposed because I didn't want them looking at me like I was an idiot.

But I wasn't. So, I told myself to have some damn balls. I shared the news with my stats instructor when she asked about my grades.

"Garrett, it seems like tutoring is paying off."

She had no idea…

"It is. The course material is finally making sense. Guess I just needed that extra boost."

Instead of looking like a man-eater, she actually resembled a concerned professor, grateful that her student had turned the corner. She'd thankfully stopped hitting on me when I lied and made up a story about having a girlfriend. Now I could have an actual conversation with the woman without worrying whether she was going to start tearing her clothes off. Or mine.

"Part of the issue is that I'm dyslexic."

I spoke the words as if I said them every day. But on the inside, my stomach was churning. I couldn't deny it. I'd spent so many years hiding it from all but the few people who absolutely had to know. Taking the risk of making it common knowledge was going to feel uncomfortable for a long time. But that was okay. I could survive outside the comfort zone.

And to my surprise, my instructor was unfazed.

Later, Franki wanted some background. "Why'd you keep it to yourself for so long?" she'd asked.

So many reasons.

"You know what they do with kids who have learning disabilities, right? They assume they are all exactly the same, and throw them into remedial classes."

And god knew I'd been in more than my fair share

of those until my parents wised up and approached the school board at the beginning of every school year with boxing gloves on. It must have been exhausting, year after year, to advocate for a kid who wanted nothing more than to be in a mainstream classroom.

"I'd never really thought about it," she said quietly, reaching for my hand over the dining table in my dorm suite.

I shrugged. "And why would you? It's kind of a hidden tragedy, the way a lot of LD kids are treated."

The look on her face about slayed me.

It wasn't one of pity, or even sympathy, but more like acceptance, like she was walking alongside me and my challenge. I felt understood. Not judged.

And it was awesome.

"Are you going to tell your coach?" she asked.

I'd been thinking about that, too. It felt *really* risky. Maybe the biggest risk of them all.

"I... I'm not sure yet. I don't know if it could have an impact on my scholarship. And my playing. I might be okay now, but when they were recruiting, well I was ready to do almost anything to keep it under wraps," I said.

I tossed my stats book closed, somehow twisting just the wrong way, and a sharp pain screeched through my shoulder.

"Shit," I said, stumbling from the agony.

"Oh my god," Franki said, extending her arms.

As if she could catch me.

I leaned onto the table while the pain dissipated. "I'm fine. I just wasn't expecting that. Whew. Took my breath away."

She took the hand from my good side and led me to the sofa in our small living room.

I knew I had to do something about my damn shoulder. But that would mean being benched for one or possibly more games. Fuck if I wanted that to happen.

"What does the coach say about this shoulder problem?"

"He has no idea. Are you kidding?"

She scrunched up her face in disbelief. I didn't blame her. She didn't know much about playing sports at my level—not that there was any reason she should. But she was learning that the disincentives to being open about injuries were never ending.

"Okay. Educate me. Why would you not take care of an injury?"

Ah, logic. Unfortunately, college sports were anything but.

"Your question makes perfect sense. But I'd have to take time off playing, and I don't want to miss any games. It's not a career-ending type of injury, so I'm willing to risk it for the reward of playing."

When I said it out loud, I realized how crazy my justifications sounded. And I didn't even bring up my concerns over letting the rest of the team down, or feeling like a wimp. Silly maybe, but they were real issues that every player dealt with.

Athletes were supposed to be strong. Superhuman, even. Since I'd started playing as a little kid it had been drilled into my head that I needed to be tough. I couldn't count the number of times I'd gotten hurt and just *sucked it up* by taking a couple aspirin and hoping for the best.

Franki shook her head slowly. "This is all so foreign to me. It seems that if you are hurt, you do something to get better. Not get out on the field and possibly get even more messed up. I'd hate to see that happen to you, Garrett."

I turned to her and put my hands on either side of her face, careful to favor my achy shoulder. I never knew when the damn thing would zap me with its agony, leaving me gasping as the waves of pain peaked and then subsided.

And fuck if Franki wasn't more beautiful every time I saw her. Earlier in the day, it was all I could do to keep from running to her like a damn fool, and god knows I chased off that skinny creep from the tutoring center so fast the guy's head was spinning.

Now she was in my arms. I pulled her closer, until our mouths collided, and tasted her delicious lips, something I'd been thinking about since the last time we'd kissed.

I knew she'd been with Zane and Atlas, and I wasn't bothered one bit. That is, as long as she made time for me. I wasn't a possessive guy.

Luckily, the other two didn't seem to be, either.

I slipped the blouse off her shoulders and leaned back to take in the sexy lace bra that cupped her tits just so, like an offering I hadn't realized I'd been hungry for. And as if she knew exactly what I needed, she reached behind her back and unhooked the garment, tossing it aside so I could reach her warm flesh.

"Hey. What's going on here?"

Both our heads snapped in the direction of Zane's voice. He stood in the doorway to his bedroom, wearing nothing but a white towel wrapped around his waist, apparently just having gotten out of the shower.

I'd totally forgotten he was home.

"Zane," Franki said. "I can't believe there is a towel big enough for guys like you to wear."

He looked down and laughed. "You got me there. This is actually an oversized beach towel. I can't stand the little ones."

Overflowing with sexy confidence, Franki sat back on the sofa, her breasts pert and pointed, and patted the empty spot next to her. "Why don't you come join us?"

Good god. A woman after my own heart.

And not surprisingly, Zane didn't need to be asked twice.

As soon as he sat, Franki twisted in his direction and, while still holding my hand, ran her other hand up the side of Zane's face and leaned in to kiss him.

He went directly for one of her tits, and I helped myself to the other.

She moaned quietly, pulling back from Zane and turning to me.

Just as she did, there was a *rap-rap-rap* on the door.

"Guys," a low voice said. "It's me. Atlas."

"Hey, Atlas," Franki sang, holding her blouse in front of her and springing up to get the door.

Fuck, she was sexy.

She stood aside as she pulled the door open to remain out of sight, and Atlas wandered in.

"Nice," he said, smiling broadly as he took in the little party we were having. He looked at Franki. "Got room for one more?"

She dropped her blouse and ran to him. "Of course," she laughed, and planted a big kiss on his mouth.

He growled as he backed her up to the dining table, and when her ass reached it, he pushed the books all over it to the floor. He got her jeans off in record time and propped her up so she was sitting on the very edge.

Zane and I looked at each other, nodding with approval.

Then Atlas pulled out his cock, which Franki immediately wrapped her hands around. He pulled her closer, until she was almost falling off the table, and ground himself against her pussy lips.

Dude was not wasting any time.

"Baby, I think I need to be inside you," he said, pulling a condom from his back pocket and handing it to her.

She looked over her shoulder at us and smiled.

I walked over to get a better view, and Zane jumped to his feet.

"Wait. Give me just a sec," he said.

He ran into his room, returning with his wireless headphones, and placed them over Franki's ears.

She laughed as he adjusted them, and she rolled the condom down over Atlas's hard-on.

"What's she listening to?" I asked Zane.

"D'Angelo. The Voodoo album."

Nice.

Zane turned her head to kiss him at the same time Atlas plunged inside her.

Eyes closed, she swayed between them as well as the music filling her ears, her tits bouncing as Atlas gripped her ass, barely balanced on the edge of the table.

She broke away from Zane's kiss in time to release a slow moan, and my own dick popped to full attention. Letting her head drop back, she began to shake as Atlas kept pummeling her.

"Oh god," she cried. "So good… so fucking good."

With a grunt, Atlas drove into her one more time and held himself there. She draped her arms limply over his back, her head still lolling, lost in the sensation and music, and the admiration of three men who weren't quite sure what had hit them.

27

FRANKI

STILL BURIED INSIDE ME, ATLAS LIFTED ME WITH HIS giant hands and carried me over to the sofa, where I straddled him. He bounced me up and down on his dick a few more times and stopped, exhausted.

I removed my headphones and threw them aside, falling into him with my head on his shoulder.

"You good, baby?" he whispered.

All I could do for the moment was nod. And when I finally got my voice back, I lifted my head to look around the room, squinting like I'd never seen the before.

"Damn, Atlas," Garrett growled. "Looks like you fucked the stuffing out of her."

I laughed weakly. He had a point.

I waved. "I'm alive. I swear. But that was so intense, especially with the music."

Seriously. It was like I was floating in space. If space were a place where you got your brains fucked out.

"Thought you might like it," Zane said.

Two large hands landed on my shoulders, running down my arms so lightly that I shivered on Atlas's lap.

"Oh my god, that feels nice," I murmured, rolling my head around on my neck.

A kiss landed on my cheek and Garrett whispered in my ear. "I'd like to fuck you now, gorgeous. How do you feel about that?"

He should have said fuck me *again* since we'd done the deed once before. But it was understood.

I dropped my head back to look at him. Jesus, at this point he could do anything to me and I wouldn't complain.

In fact, if they *didn't* do something to me, that's when I would start to get unhappy.

"Why, Garrett, that would be lovely," I said with play-formality.

I started to unfold my legs, where I was still straddling Atlas, when Garrett gently pushed me back in place.

"No, baby, stay where you are."

On Atlas's lap?

Atlas, grinning wickedly, shrugged.

A condom snapped behind me, and Garrett put his hands on my hips, lifting me from my knees just until my breasts were in Atlas's face. Then he leaned me slightly forward over him, pushing my ass in the air. His hands traveled down my sides, settling on my waist, which he could almost completely encircle with his thick fingers.

"Fucking hot," Zane mumbled from somewhere in the room.

Garrett smoothed his hands over my cheeks, and with a gentle grip, spread me open.

For a moment, so exposed and raw, all I wanted to do was tuck myself away. But when I heard Garrett growl behind me, something bold came over me.

I was sexy.

I wanted him to see me.

I wanted them all to see me.

"Are you ready, darlin'?" Garrett asked, positioning himself at my entrance.

God, was I ready. I was nothing more than a ball of utter craving. In fact, I wanted him to fuck me so badly I pushed back against him until he was just inside me.

"Oh, baby's eager," he said.

"Fuck me, Garrett. Please," I begged.

He bounced around my pussy opening, tormenting

me until I cried out, pleading with him to give me more.

I looked down at Atlas for a moment, and saw that not only was he hard again, but he was also stroking himself from root to tip. He saw me watching and smiled, popping a kiss on my lips.

That's when Garrett plunged all the way inside me, sending me into an altogether new level of pleasure. My head dropped and we reached a tight rhythm, my breasts bumping against Atlas's face every now and then.

As I was fading in and out of reality, hands turned my head to the right. I opened my eyes to find Zane, who bent to kiss me. While he did, he directed my hand to his cock, exposed thanks to the white bath towel that had fallen away somewhere along the line.

Holy shit. I was with three guys and they were all working me in one way or the other.

I was on top of Atlas, who was stroking his cock with one hand and playing with my tits with the other.

Garrett was behind me with his giant hands enclosed around my waist, pulling me back and forth on his hard cock. Who knew that when I had my one-nighter with him weeks before, we'd end up together again?

And Zane was next to me where we kissed while I stroked his long dick.

Had I died and gone to heaven? Because it sure felt like it.

Until recently, I'd never been with two guys, let alone three, and if I'd known it was going to be this fucking hot, I would have tried to make it happen a lot sooner.

The three of us writhed and groaned, coming together and then apart again.

Garrett growled and tightened his grip on me, pulling out until he was just barely inside. When he heard my gasp of disappointment at being left empty, he drove back in, sending a tidal wave of ecstasy knocking through me. He held himself there, so deep it was almost painful. An incendiary orgasm vibrated through me so hard I wondered if the guys had felt it, too.

Garrett thrust deeply one more time and held himself there, groaning as his cock pulsed, shooting his load of cum. A moment later, Zane pushing into my hand for a final time, spurting until he collapsed onto the sofa.

"Holy fucking shit," Atlas said. "That was hot."

Hot didn't begin to describe it.

28

FRANKI

"Girl, you look tired."

I side-eyed Daniel as we walked across campus to my first-ever college football game.

I'd let the guys talk me into attending one, using the upgraded seats they had access to. I was supposed to bring Maddy, but she'd worked her way out of an invitation and was replaced by Daniel, who'd driven up for the day. It was much more fun to be with him, anyway, especially since we wouldn't have to sit in the student bleachers surrounded by barfing frat bros who'd overdone it with their rum and coke cocktails.

"I *am* tired, Dan. If it wouldn't have been rude to

185

blow off the game, I might be back in my bed right now, having a nice daytime snooze."

He threw an arm around my shoulders and jostled me like he always did. "Oh, c'mon. Where's your team spirit?"

Team spirit? Whatever that was, I was pretty sure I didn't have any. College sports were for other students. I had too little time and interest to pay any attention.

I'd only agreed to this one game out of duress. And not wanting to insult the guys.

Who, by the way, had proposed again that they all date me.

While it was freaking hot as hell to mess around with them, in what world can you pull off something like dating three men?

And yet, I hadn't stopped thinking about their proposal since they'd brought it up.

First, there was sweet Garrett, who'd worked so hard to hide his learning disability that he'd boxed himself into a corner, until he couldn't anymore. He was now experiencing the freedom of honesty, which requires guts, and doesn't come without its risks. I was moved by his bravery.

Then there was Zane, who was working his way through college, hoping he could prove himself worthy of a scholarship, always keeping a foot in the goings-on at home out of concern for his younger brother and sister. So endearing.

And then there was Atlas, born into all levels of privilege, who, when it came down to it, wasn't entirely sure he deserved any of it.

I'd been so judgmental of them, and now that I knew them better, realized maybe they'd taught me even more than I'd taught them.

Silver linings, and all that.

Daniel huffed as we neared the roar of the football stadium. And the game hadn't even begun yet. "You can be a party pooper, suit yourself. I plan to enjoy the hell out of watching those hot football players in their tight little pants pound the shit out of each other on the field. Mmmm-hmmm," he said.

He caught me rolling my eyes.

"Hey, why should you be the only one to have fun? I can guarantee you there are one or two guys on that team who would be perfect recruits to take a walk on the wild side. And I'm just the man for the job," he cackled, throwing his head back.

I admired Daniel's eternal hope of converting every hot man he met to his team.

Speaking of outrageous. "Oh my god, Dan, did I tell you the latest about my hateful, cunty roommate?"

With wide eyes, he grabbed my arm and stopped me. "You said the *C* word. You never say the *C* word. This must be big. *Feed* me."

I'm glad he was excited. Me, not so much. It had been an ugly run-in. I'd finally accepted that Maddy would resent me until the end of my days, and that there wasn't a damn thing I could do about it.

I'd come back from my fun little... session with the guys, and had been in the dorm room all of five minutes when Maddy burst in and declared—loudly—that the room stunk like sex and that I was a smelly whore.

What do you even say to that?

How's your day going?

Seriously, I was stumped for a good minute or so. And by the time I recovered, I was fucking pissed at the nut job.

"Why thank you, Maddy," I said, dripping with charm. "That's so *super* nice of you to say."

She tried to stifle a smug grin, pleased she'd gotten under my skin.

"I have a question for you," I said, all innocence. "What about the guys you bring over here for your booty calls? That's not the work of a virgin, in case you haven't heard."

Let's see what she had to say about that.

"It's different," she sniffed. "You know that perfectly well."

Um, okay. Whatever.

I turned back to my book, wishing she would die.

But she wasn't ready to drop it.

"I only sleep with one guy at a time."

Oh, okay, Virgin Mary.

I really wanted to tell her who and how many guys I fucked at one time was none of her damn business, but I didn't want to confirm or deny her accusation. So I pulled on my sweatshirt to head out to play rehearsals early.

But… not so fast.

I was running out the door, throwing things into my backpack, when I realized I didn't have my marked-up script.

The one I'd made notes on. *Important* notes on.

Maddy already had her nose buried in a book. And she never studied.

"Where's my script?"

She glanced up at me. "Huh?"

"Maddy, my script was right here on my desk. Did you take it?"

We both knew she had.

She frowned and turned back to her book. "Don't be ridiculous."

Fine. I'd just get another one.

"Are you coming to rehearsals?" I asked.

She looked at me, rolling her eyes. "As your *under-study*, I don't need to be at today's rehearsal per the director. So go have fun," she said with a wave of her hand.

"Whew, that bitch needs to have her ass kicked," Daniel said when I'd finished the story.

If only.

Having trudged clear across the State campus, we finally came upon the massive stadium parking lot like we were arriving in Oz. We stopped in our tracks and looked around, amazed by the sheer festiveness of it all. The university marching band blared in the distance, people hung out all over the parking lot at elaborate tailgate parties, and the sprawl of humanity was nearly all dressed in the school colors of purple and yellow.

"Cripes. This is really something," I said, surveying the expansive parking lot where Atlas had directed me to look for his parents' tailgate party. "He said they always park in the eighth row and raise a big flag with his jersey number on it."

Sounded kind of corny to me. Cute, but corny.

"There!" Daniel said excitedly, pointing.

We worked our way through the crowd to arrive at two side-by-side Porsche Cayenne SUVs—Atlas's mom and dad's his and hers automobiles. As an extension of their open hatchbacks, they'd roped off a little area and had tables set up offering everything from just-grilled hamburgers and hotdogs to seared ahi tuna, a giant charcuterie board with more cheeses than I could count, and a soft-serve ice cream machine in the corner.

He hadn't been exaggerating when he'd said they went all out for his home games.

A beautiful middle-aged woman approached us.

"Mimosa?" she asked hopefully, a huge pitcher in her hand.

I might not like sports, but I was pretty much sold on this tailgating thing.

After she'd hooked us up with drinks, she extended her hand. "I'm Atlas's mom, Mrs. Whitlowe. That's his dad over there, having a cigar with his buddies."

I could see how Atlas resembled his mom, especially her light brown eyes ringed with a darker circle, and her oversized smile.

When I introduced Daniel and myself, her eyes widened.

Shit, what had he told her about me?

"Franki, you're the one who's sitting with us at the game. Aren't you excited?"

I forced a big, fat, fake smile.

Cocktail in hand, Daniel wandered off in search of hunky dudes, and I fell into an easy chat with Atlas's mom.

She hooked an arm through mine and led me over to a couple lawn chairs. "Franki, I understand you're the one who is helping Atlas with his classes. I want to thank you, honey. You're doing a great job. We so appreciate it."

Simply put, she was a delight.

"Will Atlas be joining us out here?" I asked, looking around for him.

She gave a little laugh. "Oh no. At this point the

players are all sequestered in some locker room. I never see him until after the game when he's showered and changed and has done any press he needs to. And as it is, he's usually so tired he just stops by our tailgate and goes back to his dorm to sleep."

Duh. It hadn't dawned on me that Atlas couldn't go to his parents' tailgate. But it made perfect sense. This was not party time for the players.

Once we were inside the stadium, Mrs. Whitlowe shuffled spots with her husband to grab a seat next to me. I was flattered but also a little freaked.

What if I somehow let slip that I'd been… cozy with her son?

When the players ran out on the field, the stadium went wild, and no one more so than Atlas's parents. They waved their flags with his number and jumped up and down and screamed.

It was one of the sweetest things I'd ever seen.

From where we sat, the guys on the field were pretty much identical hulks of uniformed men. It would have been hard to pick Garrett, Zane, or Atlas out of the throng of players if I hadn't known their jersey numbers, which I'd typed into my phone like a little cheat sheet. But now that I could tell them apart, every time any of them was on the field, I followed them with laser precision.

The players inched up and down the field in small increments, barbarously crashing into and knocking over one another with *thuds* that could be heard all the way into the stands.

"Don't worry," Atlas's mother said, patting my knee. "It's all just part of the game."

Daniel was as horrified as I, and started shielding his eyes when the game got really ferocious.

After one play that left the crowd wild, Atlas turned toward the stands and looked straight in our direction.

His mother nudged me. "We always sit in the same seats so he can find us." She frantically waved back at him and threw him a kiss.

Then he nudged the player next to him, who I realized was Garret. From way down on the field, they waved, I'm pretty sure right at me, and then high-fived each other.

Daniel poked me in the ribs with his elbow and leaned to whisper in my ear. "Oh my god, did you see that? They were looking straight at *you*. Out of all the people in this freaking place they waved at *you*."

He was right. And I couldn't wipe the smile off my face.

He leaned close again. "Girl, you must really know how to suck some dick." He slapped his hand over his mouth and doubled over laughing.

"Very funny, asshole," I whispered back.

What wasn't funny was the next play. Some huge player from the opposing team knocked the shit out of Atlas, leaving him lying on the field.

Not moving.

My heart jumped into my throat. It got hard to breathe.

Was he even still alive?

I turned to Atlas's mom. "Oh my god, what's going on?" I cried.

She patted my leg again. "Honey, this happens all the time. Don't worry, he'll be up in a moment."

But he lay there entirely too long to not worry. When an oversized human runs you over like someone did to him, I could only imagine the number of possible injuries

But thankfully, with several players and coaches gathered around him, he eventually sat up, causing the crowd to go wild.

I'd had enough. Was there a way to make a graceful exit? I was not going to be a football fan. Not ever.

No matter how much I was a fan of three particular players.

29

ZANE

"So, have you decided what you want to do?"

I looked at Coach, considering how to answer his question.

After a lot of thought, I'd chosen to work with the school newspaper on their story about me and my gang involvement. Maybe it would help someone. Who knew.

But if it cast the team in a bad light, that would *not* be cool, especially when I was trying to impress on the coach that I deserved a scholarship for playing next year.

And that's why I was trying to get a sense of the

man's thoughts on the matter. He'd never come right out and say either way, which left me to read between the lines.

My advisor had been all over the opportunity, saying it might even *help* my chances at a scholarship once the obstacles I was working to overcome became well-known. But I wasn't sure I was comfortable manipulating the system that way.

I wanted a scholarship because I was a fucking good football player, not because anyone felt sorry for me.

My grandmother, who knew little about how college worked, and even less about the media, told me to go ahead. From her perspective, I had nothing to be ashamed of and should feel proud of what I'd accomplished.

I couldn't have done any of it without her.

When I'd just gotten into my teens, most of the other boys I knew had flocked to the local gang. It was a place to belong and feel respected in a town with little opportunity for young men.

I hadn't been interested. I was committed to school and helping out at home. Until I realized that the only way to keep myself safe was by joining.

When it came down to it, you were either with the guys in the gang or against them. There was no neutral territory. And if you were against them, your well-being was in a constant state of danger.

I joined out of self-preservation.

I'm not proud of it, and I'm not proud of some of the shit I did to stay in the gang and secure their protection.

We didn't do anything too egregious—mostly just car break-ins and shoplifting. Sure, it was all against the law and someone down the line had to pay for it, but I justified it by reminding myself that other gangs reveled in drawing blood with fights or worse.

But when my grandfather was on his deathbed and essentially made me promise to get my shit together, I told the guys in the gang I was *out*. They could do their worst to me. I'd reached a point where I just didn't care anymore if they beat the shit out of me. I'd recover from whatever they did, and keep committed to my studies. It didn't take a genius to realize that by studying and getting into college, I'd earn myself a permanent escape from them.

And come after me they did, although they eventually gave up when they figured I was just never coming back. By sticking to my guns, I think I'd even earned the respect of some of them.

But not after a couple miserable beatings, one of which left me with a nice scar down my face.

Did the entire student body at State need to hear this story? Probably not. But the weaselly little reporter who'd sniffed out my past had made it clear he was going to write about me whether I wanted him to or not. By participating, I could have input on the story.

But I had to wonder if he was on to something else I *really* wanted to keep private—my involvement with Franki.

We guys had proposed that she date us—all of us—and while she'd looked at us like we were crazy, I could see she was intrigued. And a little more than turned on. But I couldn't blame her if she said no. It was an unusual sort of arrangement, and it was one that we might be able to keep secret for a while, but certainly not for the long run.

But hey, college was all about experimenting, right? If someone had a problem with our lifestyle, fuck them.

I didn't know how Franki was going to come down on the decision she needed to make. None of us did.

But we knew what we were hoping for.

So, I let the coach know the story was on. Whatever the repercussions were, if there were any, I'd deal with them.

I'd dealt with a lot worse.

30

ZANE

"Atlas, how are ya feeling?"

He was sprawled out on our suite's sofa. He opened one eye and looked my way.

"I'm good, man. Bummed I'm done for the rest of the season, but I feel pretty good. The headache is mostly gone."

That sucked. At the last game, right in front of Franki, Atlas had gotten sacked big time and ended up with a concussion. He was done for the season.

I wished that hadn't been Franki's introduction to football.

"Well, at least there were only a few games left. It could have been worse."

"Seriously. Like it could have happened at the first game. Now *that* would have sucked," Garrett added.

Everyone was quiet for a moment, reflecting on how little it took to end a player's season early—or permanently. We'd all been playing long enough to have seen random injuries mean someone couldn't play for a long time, or even ever again. Those sorts of things were devastating, but also part of the game.

It's why I always had a backup plan.

Sure, I wanted to play football because I liked it and I also hoped it would finance my education, but my long-term plan was medicine. I had no interest in the pros, not that I was good enough anyway. And any of the guys on the team who would listen to me—and there were not many them, unfortunately—got a regular lecture on planning for a post-football career.

"At least now, I can sleep in and even enjoy my life a little," Atlas said.

Funny. He seemed like he enjoyed life whether he was benched or not.

"Will your parents still be coming to the games?" I asked, wondering what it was like to have a supportive mother and father.

He nodded. "Oh yeah. I thought they'd be upset I was out of the game for a while, but they were totally cool. And they'll still go to all the games. You want them cheering for you, don't ya? You'll never have bigger supporters than my parents."

His family was worlds different from mine. It was nice to see.

Although, things at home seem to have settled down according to my mother and siblings. Dad had landed a job as a roofer and seemed to like it. It looked like this one might last, at least for a while.

"Your parents are awesome, Atlas. Hey, what did they say about Franki?" I asked.

Atlas pushed himself to sitting. "Dude, my mom loved her because she's helping me get a good grade in stats. She has no idea we... like her, you know?"

"What would she say if she did know?" Garrett asked.

He shrugged. "My parents like a smart girl. They're always warning me off the groupies, so someone like Franki would be right up their alley. You know what I mean?"

There was a knock at our suite door, and Garrett pulled it open.

There stood the lovely Franki.

"Hi, guys," she said with a brilliant smile. "Ready when you are."

We got to our feet and headed out to the training center. Coach wanted to meet the woman who'd helped the three of us turn around our grades, so we'd set up a time to show her where we spent so much of our lives.

The four of us made our way across campus, turning heads like we always did. It was one thing when a guy like me walked around by himself, but when there were three of us hulks together, we really got a lot of attention. Along the way, we were stopped a few times for photos, and a couple people took a moment to tell Atlas they were glad he was okay. It was nice, the support we got from fellow students.

And Franki enjoyed seeing us in our element.

"Coach, I'd like you to meet Franki Crawford," I said when we'd arrived at the training center.

Coach got up from behind his desk, hitched up his pants like he always did, and extended his hand to our girl.

"It's very nice to meet you, Miss Crawford. You've done an amazing job with my players here. I wanted to thank you."

She beamed. Tutoring was not a glamorous job, and we wanted her to know how she was appreciated.

"You're very welcome, Coach Jenkins," she said with her brilliant smile. "It's been my... pleasure."

Um, yeah.

But if Coach suspected anything, he didn't let on. Instead, he grabbed his briefcase and jacket and headed for the door.

"I'll see you guys bright and early tomorrow morning. Miss Crawford, enjoy seeing the training facility. It's a pretty nice one."

And he was gone.

"Wow," Franki said, "what a sweet man."

The guys and I looked at each other and laughed. "*Sweet* is not a word I think of when I envision Coach, but I can see why you'd say that," Garrett said.

Atlas nodded. "Yeah, he's sweet to *you*. He is not sweet to *us*."

"Boo-hoo," Franki said sarcastically.

"Okay, smarty pants," I said, taking her hand. "Let's show you around."

We started with the weight room.

"Oh my god, this is so fancy," Franki said, wide-eyed.

I'd been pretty dumbfounded myself the first time I saw the place. My high school had nothing on the elite training facility I now got to work out in. In fact, I was getting a little spoiled. Unless I could someday have my own home gym, after football was over, I'd never see such a nice setup again.

"Hey guys," Franki said, scouting the place, "is anyone else here?"

Her eyes were twinkling, and we knew what that meant.

Damn.

"Let me go check," Atlas said.

"If everyone's gone, lock the door, dude," Garrett

called after him. Then, he moved over to where Franki stood, and with his hands cupping her head, looked down on her.

"Why'd you want to know if anyone else was around? Are the three of us not enough for you?"

Her mouth dropped open. "On the contrary," she said flirtatiously. "I wanted to make sure we were alone."

Atlas re-joined us with a thumbs up.

Cool. Everyone else was gone, and it was time to have a little fun.

Without warning, Franki took Garrett by the hand and led him to a weight bench where she took a seat and positioned him standing right before her.

Holy shit. Was she going where I thought she was?

She reached for his belt and fly and in seconds had his erection in her hand.

He, of course, had an ear-to-ear grin, and when she brought him to her mouth, his head fell back. His groans echoed off the walls.

"Damn. Fucking hot, huh?" Atlas said, nudging me.

No kidding.

There sat our beautiful girl, right in the middle of the weight room, sitting on a bench and licking Garrett's cock like it was a popsicle.

"Dude, I am so getting in on that action," I said, unzipping my own fly and walking over to Franki.

Garrett's eyes opened when he realized I'd taken up

residence right next to him. "Oh man. You gonna let Franki have a little taste there, Z?"

I looked down at Franki, who'd just swallowed Garrett as deeply as she could. "Hell yeah," I said, pulling my hard dick out and directing it toward her.

She pulled Garrett out of her mouth and, while she kept him in her fist, took a hold of my hard-on, running her lips down it until I'd disappeared between her gorgeous lips.

I looked over at Atlas, who gave us a thumbs-up.

"Baby," I said to Franki as I watched her deep throat me, "do you think you could handle a third cock? Atlas is over there, and I hate for him to be left out."

She laughed and looked his way just in time for him to pull a sad face. She gestured with her chin that he join us and as soon as his cock was out of his pants, she began stroking him, too.

Fuck me. Our girl was serving all three of us, with me buried in her mouth and her hands on Garrett and Atlas. I'd never seen anything like it. Her eyes were half closed, and she was making soft moaning noises. I was pretty sure she was enjoying herself at least as much as we were.

When she increased her speed, I felt my balls tighten and a moment later I exploded in her mouth. Damn if she didn't manage to swallow almost every drop. And just as she released me, Garrett started to growl. She went down on him just in time to catch his load, and when he was done, she turned to Atlas, who she'd just jerked off with her hand, and caught the last of his eruption.

Holy fucking shit.

I ran to get a towel for Franki, covered in cum as she was. We wiped her clean and helped her to her feet, wobbling as we did.

"How you feeling, baby?" I asked her.

She just smiled.

I got it. We felt the same.

31

FRANKI

"Why don't you come with me? It will be fun."

It took about all the grace I had to invite Maddy to the party the guys were having, but I'd been looking to extend an olive branch.

A lot of good it did.

She sniffed but didn't even look up from her laptop. "When is it?"

"Tomorrow."

"Where?" she asked.

"At the guys' dorm."

She slammed her laptop closed, grabbed her bag,

and headed for the door. "I'll have to let you know," she mumbled, and pulled the door closed behind her.

She was heading to play rehearsals. And no, she wasn't interested in walking with me.

Ugh. What a bitch. I knew I shouldn't have bothered trying, she was that insufferable. But the guys had suggested it. They figured they could point her out to a couple other guys from the team who could chat her up and make her feel good about herself.

Who knew three college football players would be more charitable than I was?

I reached under my bed for my Pride and Prejudice script, where I'd hidden it out of view of Maddy, and went to my closet for a jacket to protect against the cool Fall air.

But… my jacket was gone.

Really?

Had that psycho actually taken to messing with my clothes?

Rage blew through me, and I yanked her closet doors open with the fantasy of shredding each of her cashmere sweaters with a sharp pair of scissors.

But I didn't.

I dug into my dressers for a second sweatshirt, pulled it over my head, and hustled off to rehearsals as puffy as the Michelin man.

After I arrived at the theater and was waiting for the director to get things started, I noticed a couple surreptitious glances my way from the rest of the cast.

I walked up to the guy playing Mr. Darcy. "Hey. Do you have any idea why people are looking at me?"

Embarrassed, he avoided my eyes. "Um, well. Maddy... said some things."

Oh, for Christ's sake.

I didn't know what she'd told people, but I could guess. On one hand I didn't care. This was a theater group and people lived their lives however they wanted. But on the other hand, she'd gone too far.

It was time to take action.

The question was—what action should I take, short of pushing her in front of a speeding train?

I decided to have a talk with the director.

"Hi, Franki. What's up?" he asked, looking up from his laptop.

I took a deep breath and looked at the empty theater seats behind him. They gave me a sort of comfort, bringing me back to warm memories of the plays I'd done in high school, and the complete and total satisfaction I'd gotten out of acting. Why had I let my parents talk me out of pursuing it? I might be hitting a bump in the road at the moment with all the Maddy bullshit, but I couldn't remember ever being happier than when I was on a stage.

Except for maybe when I was with Garrett, Zane, and Atlas.

Focus girl.

"Hey, I noticed when I came to rehearsals today that I was getting a lot of looks from everybody. Apparently, people are talking about me. I wanted to level with you and see if you had any concerns."

Looking down, he took a deep breath, then met my gaze. He was a good guy who I had a lot of respect for. The last thing I wanted was to make his job more difficult.

"Yeah, I heard some rumor about you and the football team. I'm glad you brought it up. Listen, I could give a damn what you do in your private time, but who do you think is trying to make you look bad? We can't have that be part of our production. It's a distraction, and gossip hurts morale. I won't have it."

I didn't blame the guy.

I hesitated to throw Maddy under the bus. I usually preferred to fight my own battles. But this was different.

I lowered my voice. "It was Maddy. I mean, I'm pretty sure it was Maddy. She's mad I got the role she wanted."

He nodded. "Isn't she your roommate?"

"Yup."

Sad, but true.

"Okay. I'm glad I know what's going on now. Let's get to rehearsals."

I put my hand on his arm. "Thank you. Thank you for your support and, well, everything."

He patted my hand and we got to work.

But not without issues.

I couldn't deny that I was upset the rest of the *Pride and Prejudice* cast had been told some shit about me by someone wishing me harm. They were all good people, the cast and crew, and I know they weren't judging me. But it still didn't feel good.

Because of that, I was damned if I could remember my lines. I usually had no trouble with memorization, but today was another story.

And to make matters worse, when I flubbed, there was someone in the wings snorting and making smart-assed remarks.

Thanks, Maddy.

"Someone needs to spend more time studying her lines and not pulling trains with football players," she mumbled in the distance.

The guy playing Mr. Darcy looked offstage with wide eyes.

Shit. Now everyone was distracted.

So what did I do?

Flubbed my lines again.

And the result was another rude, smart-assed remark. *"Oh my god. They never should have given her that role,"* she sniped.

Great. Now I was getting a lump in my throat, and I

couldn't say anything. Mr. Darcy looked at me with a little nod, as if he would wring my lines from me.

But it was no good.

The director stormed onto the stage. "Everybody, take five."

He walked straight to me. "I'll take care of this. Just give me some time."

The question was, did *I* have time?

My lead in the play was one thing. But my job at the counseling center was the financial foundation of my education.

No way could I afford to lose that if her rumors spread further.

32

FRANKI

"HAVING FUN WITH YOUR *FOOTBALL STARS*?"

As if talking trash about me to the cast and crew of *Pride and Prejudice* weren't enough, Maddy had apparently gotten to Max, the director of the tutoring center, who was by now no longer a fan of mine, at least since Garrett had given him a good shaking up.

I decided to ignore the snark in his voice. "The guys are doing great. They've all brought up their grades. I'm feeling pretty good about that."

I thought if I were positive, maybe he'd see the guys' success as a positive reflection on the tutoring center, and then on himself.

"Yeah well, that's what you get paid for." He sniffed. "Just watch yourself. I don't want you getting a bad… reputation or anything." With a smirk, he turned and slithered back to his office.

So that was how it was going to be.

How the hell did I get in this situation, with piss ants like Maddy and Max having some sort of unearned ability to fuck with my life?

All I wanted to do was get my college education without taking on a mountain of debt. Was that so much to ask?

I had some hard choices to make.

And as much as it made me want to vomit, I knew my first step was to call things off with the guys.

My dalliances with them, as private as I'd tried to keep them, were beginning to cause problems and I knew that, given time, they would be trouble for them, too.

Plus, since their grades had come up, to be honest, they didn't even need me anymore. I'd given them a good foundation for their stats class, and during our sessions these days, I pretty much just watched them fly through their study practice problems so we had time for other more… interesting things.

Not that I was complaining.

But my work with them was done.

In fact, to escape all the bullshit drama swirling around me, I was seriously thinking about leaving

State. I could just transfer to another school and start over without the baggage of 'having pulled trains' as both Maddy and Max had so nicely put it.

Yeah. That's what I could do.

I dialed *home*.

"Mom, I might transfer to another school next year, for junior year. Don't worry, I won't choose an expensive one."

I heard chairs scraping in the background and knew my mom was taking a seat at the kitchen table to chat. I could see her now, setting aside the New York Times crossword and doodling on her ever-present notepad.

"Funny you called, Franki. I was just going to call you, and about the same subject."

Oh shit. This didn't sound good. While they hadn't been able to foot the whole bill for my education at State, they had pitched in what they could, and it was enormously helpful.

If that money were gone, I supposed I could always take on more tutoring students. But that meant I'd have to deal with Max, and maybe even more football players, since they now knew I was good at what I did.

Wasn't this exactly what I was trying to get away from?

And even if I transferred, wouldn't I be facing the same challenges? Well, minus the train-pulling bullshit.

"Mom, I was thinking—"

But she cut me off. "Before you say anything, honey,

I wanted to let you know your father's and my situation has changed a bit."

I gulped. This was going to be bad.

Real bad.

"Um, what do you mean?" I choked.

"It's so crazy," she said breezily, "but they want your dad back at the office for another couple years. At first he said no, because we had our RV plans and so forth, but they offered him a huge raise, and he didn't want to turn it down. I didn't really want him to take it but…"

Mom prattled on while I tried to read between the lines of what she was saying.

Okay, dad was going back to work.

They were postponing their travel.

Might they be in a position to help out a bit more with my college bills?

Or was I being a selfish shit who should just continue to pay as much of my own way as possible?

"…so, we can afford it now."

Huh?

"Sorry, Mom, um, you cut out for a moment," I lied. I wasn't going to tell her I was imagining what my dad's going back to work would mean for me.

That would be over the top self-centered.

And yet.

"Could you say that again?" I asked.

She sighed. "I said, we can afford to send you to any school you want. You don't have to stay at State."

Holy shit.

Had she just said what I thought she'd said?

That would solve all my problems and then some.

No more State.

No more tutoring.

No more worrying about money.

And no more accusations of 'pulling a train.'

It was amazing how the small things could make a big difference.

For a moment, my heart soared. And then it sank. Those were all big freaking changes. And the biggest one of all?

No more Garrett, Zane, or Atlas.

But that was what I wanted. Wasn't it?

33

ATLAS

"I HAVEN'T SEEN HER. HAVE YOU?"

I scanned the crowd. It was early yet, and already our party was looking to be a huge success. But I wasn't surprised. When you're on the football team, you know a lot of people. They might not necessarily be friends, but they were usually fun enough to invite to a party. Between the three of us and the rest of the guys on our floor, we filled almost the entire dorm. The part of the crowd that couldn't fit indoors had spilled all over our front yard and even partially into the street.

The cops would arrive at some point. But hopefully not until well into the party.

"I haven't seen her either," I told Garrett. "Shall we call her?"

Yeah. We were waiting for Franki. *Impatiently* waiting.

He nodded. "I'll go outside. It's too loud in here."

He'd disappeared into the crowd to push his way outdoors when I found Zane.

"Killer party, huh?" I said.

"Seriously. You know who that blonde over there is?" he said.

Was he kidding? The damn party was full of blondes.

I followed his gaze over the crowd and settled on a girl who looked like she was holding court with her friends. They were gathered around her, listening intently.

I could only imagine what she was blathering on about.

"Is that her? The pretty one?"

He nodded. "Yeah. That's Franki's roommate. She pointed her out when we were walking across campus a while back."

I was surprised Zane could remember her after seeing her just once. She looked like every other good-looking girl at State, especially the ones that chased after football players. But I guess after the stories

Franki had told us about her, it was a face you didn't let yourself forget.

And now here she was at our party, which Franki had been nice enough to invite her to. But Franki herself was nowhere to be seen.

"Let's see if she knows where Franki is."

He nodded, and I led the way through the crowd.

I tapped the blonde on the shoulder. "Hey, are you Franki Crawford's roommate?" I asked.

She whipped around and before she answered she looked back at her friends with an 'I've got this' glance.

She flipped her hair back and looked me up and down. Then she licked her lips and shrugged with one shoulder. "Yeah. I am. At the moment, anyway."

She looked back at her posse, and they all giggled.

Was she for real?

"Do you know where she is?" I asked.

She rolled her eyes. "Do I look like her babysitter?" she scoffed.

Okay.

She was worse than I'd thought.

I turned back to Zane, and we started to walk away when she grabbed my arm.

"Hey, where are you going? You need to meet my friends and me," she flirted.

A giggle ran through the group again.

Jesus. She was exactly the kind of girl I *didn't* want to meet.

But I decided to fuck with her.

"Okay. And what's your name?" I asked.

She extended her hand like she was doing me a big favor. "I'm Maddy. Maddy Browne. And you don't have to introduce yourselves. We know who you both are."

The girls tittered again.

"Well, nice meeting you. We'll see you later," I said, and we turned to leave.

I watched her long enough to see her smile fall, and her expression turn into one of disgust.

And apparently, we didn't walk away fast enough.

"*Those* are the guys who Franki is fucking. Can you believe it, that they'd go for a slut like her? I mean, girls, aren't *we* the type that these guys should go after?"

Did she really just say that?

I turned back around to tap Maddy again, who apparently didn't realize we were still within earshot.

Her eyes widened.

"That was a really nasty thing to say."

She faltered for a moment, then got her fake face back on. "Oh, um, I was just kidding." She dropped her head back and tried to laugh breezily.

And unsuccessfully.

I looked at Zane, and he nodded.

I took Maddy by the upper arm. "You need to leave. Right now."

She scowled and tried to shake me off. "What? Are you kidding?"

"I wish I were kidding, lady. Now get the hell out."

I started dragging her toward the door, and not surprisingly, her friends fell right into line. When I got them outside, I let her go.

"And don't come back," I called, waving goodbye as I watched all their mouths hang open.

Consequences were a bitch.

When we were back inside, Garrett caught up to us.

"Hey. What was that all about?" he asked.

We filled him in, and he laughed.

"Damn. I bet they didn't see that coming," he said.

And none of us saw what was coming next, either.

34

ATLAS

"Hey, you made it."

I bent to kiss Franki, but she turned her head in time for me to catch her temple. Which was fine. I got that she probably didn't want everyone at the party in her business.

"Yeah. Hey, is there someplace where we could all go for a couple minutes? I have something to discuss."

The guys and I looked at each other, and I knew what we were hoping.

C'mon baby. Give us some good news.

We followed her to Zane and Garrett's suite since mine was too small for the four of us to fit into.

I started to take a seat when we got there, but Franki stood by the door, not even coming in all the way.

What the hell.

"I… I don't know how to say this, so I'm just going to get right to the point," she started.

Well shit. This didn't sound good. At all.

"I'm leaving State. I'm transferring to a new school."

"What? Why?" Garrett asked.

She looked down at her shoes and shook her head before she looked back at us, each one at a time. "I… I don't think our being together is good for me… or you. I just… can't do it. And my parents said they'd pay for me to go somewhere else. I'm really sorry."

She turned and ran out the door. If the three of us hadn't been so shocked, we probably would have run after her.

"Holy shit. What the hell was that?" Zane asked, finally getting up and looking into the hallway—as if she might still be there.

Instead, I ran to the window and saw Franki jogging back toward her own dorm.

And just like that, it was over.

Or was it? After all, it never really got started.

"Goddamn," Zane said. "Just when I thought things were looking up."

He sat, slowly shaking his head, staring off into space.

I'd never seen him like that.

"What do you mean?" I asked.

"I got word from Coach that I'm in for a scholarship next year. Junior year is covered for me, and most likely senior, too."

Holy shit.

"Dude, that's great news," I said.

But he didn't look too happy.

"It is great news. I'd been psyched about sharing it with you guys and Franki tonight. I really thought shit had turned a corner. And now she's gone, leaving for another school? What the fuck?" he said. "I finally thought I'd be able to breathe easier."

Instead, he looked like he could barely breathe at all.

I could relate. For a moment, I, too, felt like someone had belted the air out of my chest. As if I'd just been tackled by someone twice my size.

Instead, I'd been floored by someone *half* my size.

And as a new reality settled in for all of us, we each sat quietly with our thoughts while a huge party raged on just a few feet away.

The party didn't matter anymore.

Nothing seemed to.

I'd learned a lot this semester, not least of which was the unappealing subject of statistics.

But I'd also picked up a thing or two about priorities. Maybe some of the things I'd thought were important before, really weren't.

It was never too late to learn something new.

Was it too late to explain that to Franki?

35

FRANKI

"It's nice to see you again, Miss Crawford."

I took in the benevolent face of the university's football coach, who was dressed in a polo-style short-sleeved shirt. A windbreaker was draped on the back of his desk chair where he sat, and a baseball cap sat on the corner of his desk. According to the guys, removing hats indoors was something Coach was a stickler about

I'd always thought coaches were just grown-up jocks, but I was getting the feeling they were more than that. Teachers, mentors, surrogate dads.

It was something, this world I knew so little of until

recently—which I'd been dragged into kicking and screaming.

"Nice to see you again, Coach."

He'd reached out to set up a meeting, and while I had no idea why, I'd said yes right away. But I was nervous. Now that I was sitting there in front of him, it was all I could do to force a smile.

I glanced down at my hands, clasped together so tightly my knuckles were turning white, and decided to hide them under my thighs.

"How's your semester going?" he asked with a grandfatherly smile.

I shook my head enthusiastically. "Really well. Grades are looking good and I got the lead in the drama department play."

His eyebrows rose. "Really? What play?"

"Jane Austen's *Pride and Prejudice*," I said proudly.

I loved saying those words.

He nodded slightly. "Oh yes, my late wife loved Jane Austen."

"Yes, Jane Austen is my favorite," I gushed.

He nodded kindly. "Well, Miss Crawford—"

"Oh, you can call me Franki."

His eyes crinkled. "Franki—I want to thank you for the great job you've done with the boys. Their progress has been incredible."

I felt a slight heat wash over my face, and realized I was blushing.

Jesus, get it together, girl.

"It's been my pleasure. They are smart guys. They just needed a stronger foundation to build on."

He nodded. "I knew they could pull it off, they just needed some support. Now, there's another thing I wanted to bring to your attention."

Oh. Shit. And I'd been feeling so great.

My stomach shared its displeasure with a nauseating churn, and I held my breath, waiting for some kind of accusation, given those I'd faced in recent days.

What had he heard?

He leaned forward, hands clasped, and rested his arms on his desk. "Someone came to me and told me you were doing the guys' homework for them and even managed to take a test or two for them."

What?

The churn in my stomach? It was now roiling in the middle of my chest, getting closer to my throat. I scrambled for my backpack where I had a couple sips left in my water bottle. The cool liquid provided a modicum of relief. But I had a feeling it wouldn't last.

I didn't need to puke in front of the university's head football coach.

And what did he mean 'someone came to him?' For fuck's sake. What was with the goddamn mystery? We all knew who it was.

As my eyes threatened to fill with tears, I looked around Coach's office, littered with the chunky acrylic awards men liked to give each other for jobs well done, several covered with sticky fingerprints and the ones beyond cleaning reach drowning in layers of dust. As my rage built, I saw them as garish reminders that I'd fallen into a world that was not my own, and where I didn't belong.

I wanted to swipe them off their shelves and watch them crash to the floor where they'd make a huge mess that I didn't have to clean up.

As kind as Coach's face was, I wanted to tell him to fuck off. I wanted to tell everyone to fuck off. Leave me alone. Get out of my way and let me get my goddamn education.

"I hope you know that is complete and utter bullshit," I said.

Coach's eyes widened, and I wasn't sure who was more surprised at my outburst. The words had come flying out of my mouth like verbal diarrhea. But I didn't care, they portrayed how I felt.

This was some serious shit, and I wasn't downplaying the strong feelings I had about it.

"I know, Franki. I believe you. For one, it's virtually impossible to take a test for someone else in a small classroom. The teacher would know. And just the fact that the guys obviously did take the tests themselves, and did well on them, proves you didn't do their homework for them either."

Okay. So he knew it was bullshit, too.

But why even bring it up, then?

"I've worked with high profile students all my coaching career. They attract a lot of attention, and not all of it good. This is par for the course. I'm just sorry you got involved."

Yeah. No shit.

"Look," he said, "these things come out of jealousy. We know that. Someone resents the relationship you have with the guys, which I was told is more than just a professional one."

The roiling was back.

But this time I'd had enough. I swept my backpack off the floor and stood to leave.

I didn't need this. Not one bit.

But Coach held up his hand. "Hang on, Franki. You are all consenting adults. What you do together is your business. My only desire was to see the guys' grades come up, and you more than delivered. What I wanted to ask was if you're available next semester? I'd love to make sure we snap up your services before the tutoring center assigns you to someone else."

Oh. Well, then.

I slipped back into my seat. "I... I will actually be at a new school next semester. Not sure which one yet. I need to kick off the application process."

His eyes widened. "Oh, you're leaving State. Okay then. I guess that takes care of that. Can I ask why you're leaving?"

Ugh. The reasons were so many.

"Well, my parents' financial situation recently improved, so I can go somewhere more...."

More what? Prestigious? Expensive?

He nodded. "I get it. No need to explain further. My best to you, Franki."

He extended his hand and led me to the door.

Whew. For a moment, I felt a huge weight lift from my shoulders.

But the sensation didn't last.

For some reason, I felt more burdened than ever.

Why did I feel so shitty when things were supposedly falling into place?

36

FRANKI

"I'VE BEEN TOLD I NEED TO APOLOGIZE TO YOU."

I glanced up from my laptop to find Maddy peering down at me. I quickly looked her up and down to make sure she wasn't holding any sharp objects, and when I realized I was relatively safe, I was able to think about her words.

Like, what the hell?

How does someone go from hating your guts and spreading all kinds of smack around, to freaking apologizing?

"Maddy, what's behind this?"

She plopped down in her desk chair and turned it

to face me. "I've been kicked out of the play. The director told me I was out, that they'd find another understudy for your role, and that I couldn't participate in another production until next semester at the soonest."

Holy shit.

"He also told me to apologize to you or I'd be out of the drama department permanently."

Ah. Okay.

"So you're only apologizing because you have to. Okay. I get it."

She pressed her lips together. "I guess… this was a wakeup call. It made me realize what a psycho bitch I've been. I'm sorry. You did nothing wrong." Her voice broke.

Yeah. Her voice actually fucking broke.

Maybe she should have gotten the role of Elizabeth Bennett because she was turning out to be a pretty good fucking actress.

"Why did you do it?" I asked in a small voice.

She put her hand over her face and rubbed her eyes. "Things always seem so easy for you. I was jealous."

Okay, she really was crazy.

"Things are easy for *me*? How the hell did you get that impression? Because I can assure you, you are wrong."

"You're so confident in who you are, and you have such a cool style…"

I looked down at my jeans with the knee-hole, and my dirty Converse Chucks. I rubbed my eyes and a snowfall of old, black mascara rained down on my shirt.

Um, *style?*

I didn't trust her. Who knew, maybe she was setting me up like the psycho she'd proved herself to be.

I turned back to my computer. "I'm leaving State, anyway. So thanks for apologizing, but I'll be out of your hair soon enough."

God, those words choked me. What the hell was that about? I was finally getting what I wanted. Right?

"I don't blame you if you hate me," Maddy said in a wobbly voice. "What I did was wrong. I knew it was wrong when I was doing it. I'm… embarrassed. And ashamed."

I looked at her again. The heaviness in her eyes *looked* sincere. I wasn't completely sold, though she should be both embarrassed *and* ashamed.

"The thing is, Franki," she continued, "people really *like* you."

Oh. Okay.

"And they respect you," she added.

I didn't feel very fucking respected when she'd trashed me to the cast and crew of our play.

"I said some terrible things about you. And you know what I learned?"

I was afraid to find out.

"I learned that no one believed my bullshit because they knew the kind of person you were. And you know one more thing?"

Jesus. I appreciated her apology. But how many more clarifications did she need to offer?

"Personally, I think you'd be crazy to throw all that away."

Well. Some people would say I was crazy to *not* throw it all away.

37

GARRETT

Blown away was the only way to describe it.

Atlas, Zane, and I—and Franki's friend from home, Daniel—sat in the third row of the campus performing arts theater to watch opening night of *Pride and Prejudice*.

Best seats in the house, she'd assured us—not too close and not too far from the stage.

I had to say I agreed with her.

And it was easy to see why she'd gotten the lead role.

I'd never read *Pride and Prejudice*. That kind of lovey-dovey story was not my thing. But I couldn't pass up seeing Franki, even if she had decided against being with us guys. And damn if she didn't do a bang-up job playing the smart and smart-assed second sister in the Bennett family.

I was so proud of her that during the standing ovation, I had to sneakily wipe away a tear or two. I think Daniel saw me, which was cool because he was doing the same thing.

Afterward, we three guys headed back across campus to get some sleep in preparation for a very early morning.

Franki's parents and siblings had been in attendance, too, and we figured we'd let them all go backstage and celebrate whatever it was that people did on opening night.

But we didn't do it without heavy hearts.

Our conversation was light on the walk home.

"So, your shoulder's feeling better?" Atlas asked.

Geez, it was so much better I'd almost forgotten I'd ever hurt it.

I rolled it to show my magical healing powers. "It feels pretty good since I broke down and got some physical therapy. Only once in a while when I turn a certain way does it tweak a little. The trainer's PT really worked."

I didn't want to say too much about it. Atlas was still bummed he'd have to sit out the rest of the season due to his concussion.

Actually, we were all bummed. The QB who'd replaced Atlas had thrown several interceptions in just one game that had killed our early season winning streak.

"It's gonna be weird," Zane said from out of nowhere.

Without further explanation, we knew exactly what he was talking about.

Franki's leaving.

There were still a few weeks left in the semester, and we were certainly on a friendly basis with her, but our tutoring sessions had come to an end. We'd see her around from time to time, but it wasn't going to be like it had been.

And that sucked.

In fact, after this semester, we'd probably never see her again. She was off to greener pastures. We were happy for her, of course, but still.

At least we had new living arrangements to look forward to. Atlas's loaded father had bought a little house a few blocks from campus for Atlas to spend his final couple semesters in. Lucky for us, he'd invited us to join him as roommates. The three of us had become pretty tight over the course of the semester, which was damn amazing considering where Zane and Atlas had started.

In a sense, I gave credit to Franki for bringing us all

together. She'd impacted our lives in any number of positive ways. But I couldn't focus on that now.

What was done, was done.

"I can't believe Coach is letting us move out of the dorm," I said.

"Well, you know the stipulation," Atlas said as we got back to our building.

Coach had his rules, but they were nearly always fair.

We could only live off campus if we kept our grades up. The funny thing was it was probably going to be a thousand times easier to get good grades in a quiet, three-person house. Dormitories were *not* conducive to studying.

Did people not know that?

We filed into Zane's and my room, where we'd all been hanging out lately.

Atlas kicked his shoes off and put his feet up on the coffee table. "I'm psyched. I really am. It's cool having a single room, but it's so small it was starting to drive me crazy. And it will be nice to have some quiet," he said, gesturing outside our room where a rowdy pool game in the common room was underway.

Just then, my phone buzzed.

Well, shit.

"Guys, Franki's texting me."

Confusion hit Zane's face. "Isn't she doing her opening night stuff? Like with her family and all?"

I texted her back to find out what was up.

"Huh. She wants to come by to talk with us. She asks if she can meet us in thirty minutes," I said.

We looked at each other and shrugged.

"I ain't going anywhere," Atlas laughed.

Fair enough. I texted her back that we'd be here for as long as she needed us to be.

Although hopefully her thirty-minute timeframe was accurate.

We not only had to get up very early the next morning, but, speaking for myself, I couldn't wait any longer than thirty minutes to see her.

"Hi, guys."

Franki blew in the door, her face scrubbed clean of stage makeup and her hair lopsided, I imagined thanks to the wig she'd worn in the play.

Back in her ripped jeans and Converse Chucks was just how I liked my girl.

Shit. I needed to stop thinking that way.

She wasn't *my* girl. She wasn't anyone's damn girl. Nor was she going to be.

Bouncing up and down, she looked like she might explode. It was easy to see she was riding the high of a successful opening night.

As she should. She'd done incredibly well.

I approached her with a big hug. "You did an amazing job. I'm thinking of actually reading something by Jane Austen. What a ball buster your character was."

She beamed. "Thank you. And thank you all for coming. It felt so good to have people who are important to me there tonight, and I'm really happy with how things went. And even better, the director is happy, and that never happens."

"So where'd your family and everyone go?" Atlas asked.

"Oh, they've gone home. The opening night thing was pretty brief. Just long enough to say hi and meet the rest of the cast and crew."

She looked from one of us to the other, and when I glanced at the guys, I could see we were all thinking the same thing.

While we were happy to see her, we were very curious about one thing—what the hell she was doing here.

We waited patiently. What else could we do?

"It was nice meeting your friend Daniel," Zane chimed in.

She nodded enthusiastically. "Oh yeah. He really liked you guys, too."

We continued to look at each other, hoping someone would say something.

Finally, I couldn't wait any longer. "So what brings you over here, Franki?"

I'll admit it. I was hoping for good news.

It's not like things could get any worse, anyway, could they? I mean, Franki was out of here after this semester.

"Guys, I had a couple revelations tonight. And I wanted to share them with you."

She helped herself to a chair and faced us all. "First off, the director was so happy with my performance that he suggested I switch majors. To the drama department."

Wait. What?

"Are you considering that? Because you said you're transferring to another school," I said.

She took a deep breath. "I know. That was the plan. But I realized something tonight. I have to do what is right for me. Everyone in my family has gone to fancy private schools. When I thought about it, that wasn't really what I wanted. Everyone in my family has pursued a profession. That's why I was a psych major. I figured I could be a therapist. But that's not what I really wanted, either."

"What about your parents? I thought they didn't like your being involved in theater," Atlas said.

She shrugged. "I had a talk with them. And I think the director might have taken them aside and said a few things, too."

Shit. Was this going where I hoped it would? Because it was a pretty big fucking about-face.

"So, guys. What I'm saying is that I'm staying here at State. I'm switching to the drama department. And there's one other thing."

Holy shit. Dare I hope? I held my breath.

"I'd like to be with you guys. If you'll still have me," she said tentatively.

I glanced at Zane and Atlas, and before either of them could jump to their feet, I did, and ran to Franki, picking her up and spinning her around.

She squealed and laughed. "I'm so happy! I finally made some decisions *and* I got my parents' support."

I put her down so she could catch her breath.

Zane and Atlas jumped to their feet, all smiles, and ran to her, taking turns with hugs and kisses.

What a semester it had been so far. We'd all learned a hell of a lot, and I didn't mean just statistics.

I, for one, was no longer living under the staggering weight of a secret that had shamed me all my life.

I had a learning disability.

Who fucking cared?

I could handle it. It was okay to ask for help, just like I had with my sore shoulder.

Zane had gotten his scholarship and handled that crazy newspaper article, and Atlas learned his parents would support him whether he had to sit the football season out or not.

Did we know all we needed to? Hell no.

But I was confident that with Franki by our side, we could handle most anything that life threw our way.

Did you like *Her Dirty Jocks*? Learn about the next book in the Men at Work series,
Her Dirty Archeologists

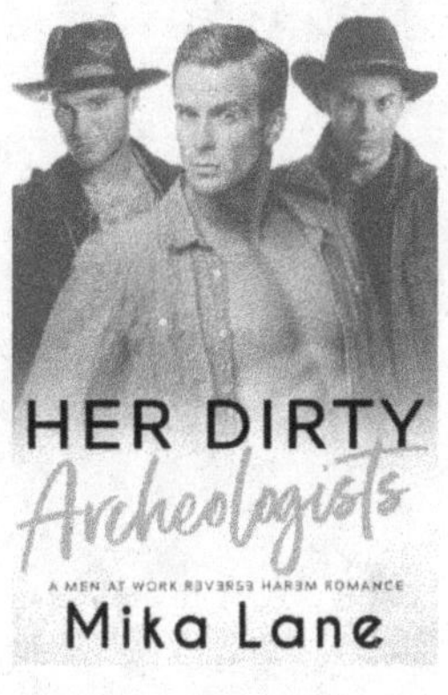

I hope you loved reading this book as much as I loved writing it. Please visit my store to learn more about my books, and to buy directly from me!
https://mikalaneshop.com/

SHOP
Mika
Lane

Dear Reader:

I'm USA TODAY bestselling romance author Mika Lane, and am OBSESSED with bringing you sassy, steamy stories with imperfect heroines and the bad-a*s dudes they bring to their knees. I'll always bring you my signature humor and heat, topped off with a modern-day happily ever after.

My first book ever was *The Day I Ate the Milkyway,* a true fourth-grade masterpiece illustrated with crayons and bound with construction paper and glue. Nowadays, steamy romance gives purpose to my days and nights as I create worlds and characters that tickle the imagination. I live in magical Northern California with my own handsome alpha dude, sometimes known as Mr. Mika Lane, and two devilish cats named Chuck and Murray.

A dual citizen of the United States and Ireland, I have on more than one occasion spent my last dollar on a plane ticket somewhere, and am always planning my next escape. I often try new recipes on unsuspecting friends, search out hiding places to read undisturbed, and sadly kill every houseplant I bring home.

I LOVE to hear from readers when I'm not dreaming up naughty tales to share. Visit my online shop https://mikalaneshop.com/ and say hello https://mikalaneshop.com/pages/meet-mika.

xoxo, Mika

www.ingramcontent.com/pod-product-compliance
Lightning Source LLC
Chambersburg PA
CBHW011200190726

48286CB00009B/2855